Lock Down Publications and Ca$h Presents

Bloody Money Bags 2

The Double Cross

Written By

KINGPEN

First Edition 2026

Printed in the United States of America

Lock Down Publications
P.O. Box 944
Stockbridge, GA 30281
www.lockdownpublications.com

Like our page on Facebook: Lock Down Publications
www.facebook.com/lockdownpublications.ldp

Stay Connected with Us!

Text **LOCKDOWN** to 22828 to stay up-to-date with new releases, sneak peaks, contests and more…

Like our page on Facebook:
Lock Down Publications

Join Lock Down Publications/The New Era Reading Group

Visit our website:
www.lockdownpublications.com

Follow us on Instagram:
Lock Down Publications

Email Us: We want to hear from you!

Chapter 1

-Big Ken-

Emmanuel said Angel's name. It wasn't that he said her name that took me by surprise. It was *how* he said it that was odd. The way it rolled of his tongue, it was like he knew her. In the past, I'd instructed Angel to meet Emmanuel to pay for my attorney fees, but that shouldn't have put them on a first-name basis. With Emmanuel being a lawyer, he should know being a professional consisted of calling people "Mister" or "Miss."

"You call my wife *Angel*, like you know her or something?"

I didn't sit down, knowing he badly wanted me to. I chose to stand up. That way, he knew I had the upper hand. I grabbed the top of the chair, making Emmanuel uneasy.

Emmanuel cleared his throat. "I think you should sit for this," he said nervously.

"I've received a lot of bad news sitting down, so just tell me, and I'll see if I can stand it or not."

Emmanuel sighed. "What I'm about to say will sound really, *really* insane." Emmanuel paused like he was in the courtroom trying to persuade the jury. I stayed silent. I had done my share of talking.

"The night your wife came to my office to make your payment . . . that night, your wife persuaded me to go with her to get the money. So, I did. She drove us to a set of apartments called *The Browns* to see a man she referred to as Dip."

When Emmanuel said my cousin Dip's name, I was all ears. He was right; I should've sat down. But then again, I'm glad that I didn't, or else Emmanuel would've seen that he had me on the edge of my seat.

"You said you went with my wife to a man name Dip's house? When was this?" I asked, just to be sure.

"It was an apartment, but yes. I was driven by your wife, and it was the day she came to make your payment."

"And what happened after she took you to see this man named Dip?" I questioned him like I was the DA and he was the one on trial.

"I witnessed something I never, ever thought I would see." The look he had in his eyes made me think he was reliving whatever he'd witnessed that night.

"I wish you would just cut the dramatic bullshit and tell me what the fuck you came to tell me," I yelled as loud as I could.

"I witnessed your wife killing Dip," Emmanuel blurted out. It was a good thing that this was a lawyer visit, or else the guards would've heard exactly what he said.

As Emmanuel's words began to sink in, I began to think about how all of it transpired. Knowing Angel, she probably had her reasons why she killed Dip. I had placed Angel in position to make the drops and pick up the money. That meant I gave her the authority to do whatever it took to get the money that was owed to us. Bu any means. My cousin Dip was no exception.

"So, you're telling me that you came all this way to tell me that you killed my cousin? I could've saved you a trip by telling you he got exactly what he deserved."

"But—" Emmanuel stuttered.

"What?" I shouted.

Emmanuel sighed. "I didn't come all this way just to tell you about the murder. I came to tell you that your wife used the murder to force me to throw your fed case."

Chapter 2

-Angel-

"*She said what you know 'bout love / I'll tell you everything. I got what you need,*" Ron sang as he danced in his jeans and tank top directly in front of me like he was a male stripper, and I was a willing tipper.

"I used to jam this shit every day in the joint, right before Pop Smoke got killed," Ron said, turning the stereo down a tad. "It's a shame how he was killed right before he was able to take the throne. In a way, it's kinda like you." He laughed. "Not that you're dead yet. But in a way, you'll die before you take the throne. Yeah, I heard Big Ken had left everything to yo' snake ass. And people call me crazy, huh?" Ron laughed to himself.

I sat in the same chair, still tied up, and my pants were still off. I had never put them back on from the last time I used the restroom. To Ron's perversion, he was loving every second of it.

"Angel, you ain't talking to me today? What's a matter?" Ron asked, his voice sounding like he was talking to a baby.

I ignored his old, ugly, perverted ass. The quicker he killed me, the better. Me not saying anything really got under his skin.

"Angel, do you know what my job is?" Ron asked, then waited like I was really going to answer.

"Well—" Ron said, walking up to me. He got on his knees right in front of me and placed his hands on my knees. My chest tightened, but I kept my composure. I knew he was trying to rattle me, and I wasn't going to let it happen.

Ron's hands caressed my knee. Being a stripper in the past I was used to a stranger's hands on me. But there was something about Ron—and what made it worse was that I was tied up, so there was no defending myself.

Ron's hands slipped up my thighs at the same time. A shiver went up my spine. His thumbs applied pressure to my inner thighs as he gripped me tightly.

"Angel, baby. I got my name in the streets back when you were probably still in your colorful polka-dot panties, still having grade school crushes. See, around that time, I was going through what you could call a phase. Now, don't get me wrong. I was a man's-man. I liked to fuck, and I liked to fuck hard, and I'm talkin' 'bout real hard. But when I caught my first body, I went home right afterwards. I was distraught. The grief of me actually killing someone set in when my wife at the time asked me who's blood was all over me. Now, I remind you, I was a street cat, and my wife knew that, so she wasn't questioning me out of concern, but out of pure curiosity."

As Ron took a drive through his troubled past, I did everything I could not to pee in the only pair of panties that I had.

"When I told my wife that I had killed her brother, she kissed me. It wasn't her favorite brother, Carl; it was her oldest brother, Damien. The one that raped her countless times as a kid. As she kissed me, she began to pull my dick out of my pants. It was so hard it damn near broke as she tried to pull it out. I fucked her so damn hard. I started choking her the harder I fucked her. She began to claw at my hands as I choked her tighter. Something in me snapped as I choked and fucked her. My wife had got aroused by her memories of her brother fucking her. So I killed her. It was something about being covered in another man's blood as I was choking her to death . . . the feeling of her thick veins under my fingers, pulsating, fighting for air. I realized as I choked her that I wasn't aroused to her pussy. I was aroused by *death*. From that day forward, the only way I've been able to get hard—the only way I've been able to get aroused—was by killing someone."

Ron leaned in to my ear and whispered: "If you'll take a look down, you'll see my dick getting hard, right . . . now."

I didn't want to, but the sick demon in me made me look. His bulge was lying on his leg. I closed my eyes in disgust.

"Now you see, Angel. Like I told you, my dick only gets hard when I'm about to kill," Ron said as he stuck his nasty tongue in my ear. I flinched as his saliva tickled my earlobe.

"Turtle, he kinda likes you. Kinda. Normally, he'll let me got to the extreme measures to get results. But you? I'm not quite sure what he has in store for you. But I can tell you this: if I'm the one to carry out the order, I assure you, when I do kill you, I'ma make love to your dead body. It's something about how a cold stiff pussy feels as you're forcing your way in and out. It's kinda like how this one time, I had to get answers from this one cat. Not sure if I told you this one before, but anyhow . . ." Ron said a she stood up and straddled me.

"I caught the guy and drugged him. I took him to the mountains, to my winter cabin. You should see it—the way it looks when it snows," he said, dazing out like he was picturing snow fall from the sky.

"So this cat—he wakes up, he's naked, except for his socks and shoes. I tied his arms around this big tree. When he wakes up, he's wondering what the fuck is going on. But the only thing he can see is the tree he's tied to. All the while, I'm sitting behind him, nice and warm with a cup of *John Wayne*."

I sat uncomfortable, fidgeting as much as I could under him. He was heavy as hell, and his breath smelled like Vienna sausages and beer. But I didn't want to piss him off, so I let him finish his story as his hard dick poke me in my stomach.

"So, when he starts talking . . . you know, '*Who's there? Where am I? Help*.' Yeah, all that. I let his naked ass scream for a while. Maybe ten minutes, until I just couldn't control myself. The urge started rising deep inside of me. He was a helpless gangster. Yelling for help, begging to be rescued. And I was the one to do it. I broke him down. Made him soft, scared of the unknown. I got more than answers from him that night. I got his virginity, and his manhood. I kept him tied to that tree for days. A pile of shit had risen by his leg from him being so afraid," Ron said as he stood up and walked to the door.

As he grabbed the doorknob, he stopped and looked back at me. He knew his story had caused a stir in me. It was the whole point of him telling it to me.

"You know, Angel, whatever comes of you, I hope I'm able to tell your story to the next person who sits in that chair." Ron snickered as he opened the door, then slammed it shut. As soon as the door slammed shut, I hung my head and peed my panties.

Chapter 3

-Big Ken-

"What's good, family? It's good to see you. I would've come down here since, but I wanted to make sure everything was everything first. Do you want something from the vending machines or som'?" Pistol asked as he sat across from me in the visitation room.

"I'm good, family. This isn't a social call so I'll pass on the zuzu's. Did you get my message?" I asked.

Pistol nodded. "Yeah, Rain hit me. I came as soon as I could. She didn't tell me much, just that you felt like some funny shit was going on."

"You don't feel it?" I asked.

"Not sure what you mean," he said.

"It gives me chills just thinking about it," I said as I rubbed my arm. "Something's not right with this whole thing. I can't quite put my finger on exactly what it is, but something's off."

"Say it, family, and I'll help you piece it all together," Pistol said.

I shook my head. So many thoughts had already invaded my mind, I didn't know if there was room for anymore. From what Emmanuel had told me and the news I received from Lluvia, it all had my mind playing tricks on me.

I sighed. I had to let some of it out. I knew what would happen if I kept it bottled up.

"Emmanuel paid me a visit the other day," I said.

"Emmanuel?" Pistol said, thinking of where the name sounded familiar. "Your lawyer?" Pistol asked.

I nodded. "Yeah."

"What the fuck did he want?"

"He came with come shit I didn't expect."

"What did he say? That he fucked you over?" Pistol laughed, obviously joking.

I nodded. As I did, Pistol's smile faded. "He did say that he fucked me over. But he wasn't alone."

Pistol slid back in his seat. "Someone helped him? What?" Pistol was confused. "Someone helped him? You mean like *someone* set you up?"

"Same reaction I had." I managed a dry laugh.

Pistol leaned forward and rested his arms on the table. "Who would be dumb enough to cross you, family?"

"Seems like my attorney . . . and my wife," I said matter-of-factly.

"I don't believe it. Are you sure?" Pistol was shocked. I nodded. "He knew shit about Dip. He knew where he stayed. And . . . he said Angel smoked him."

Pistol laughed. "Fam', what the fuck." He slammed his fist on top of the table. "Damn, fam', if I knew where she was, I would put a bullet through her skull."

"That's the problem, family. As bad as I want her dead, I want to know if she's okay."

Pistol stared at me, completely lost. "Fam. She killed our peoples—our cousin—and you're hoping she's okay? The pussy can't be that good."

"It has nothing to do with the pussy, or love," I said.

"Then what does it have to do with? Because I'm confused. This bitch sent you here, for your natural life, she killed Dip, and you gave her the reins to the ship."

"It has to do with answers. The bitch didn't wake up one morning and just say she was going to fuck a nigga over. She planned it all. And she wasn't alone. And I want to know all parties involved."

"And when you find out?" Pistol asked.

"You already know what to do. Let 'em know it came from me."

Chapter 4

-Turtle-

I sat in the backseat of the federal parking lot, watching my great-nephew exit the federal prison where my so-called protégé—my nephew, Kendrick—was being held. I watched Dieon, or as the streets called him, Pistol. To me, he was just as guilty as Angel and her snake husband, Ken. Everyone knew I'd been kidnapped, and yet no one has made the streets bleed. I'm the OG. I'm not *an* OG; to this city, I'm the only *true* OG. The Original Gangsta.

I'm still baffled that they sent a bitch to my rescue. I was tied to a chair when Bishop made the call to Kendrick to send only Angel. There was no way in hell I would've accepted that. These guys were some straight bums. They needed me alive in order to get what they wanted. If the shoe was on the other foot and it was Kendrick tied to a chair, me and my comrades would've bust through that warehouse like *The Expendables*. No questions asked. But that was before Kendrick betrayed me.

"Boss, you want me to get the second car to follow Pistol?" Ron asked from behind the wheel as he looked at me from the rear-view mirror.

"Yeah. See where he goes. Tell them to stay out of sight. I don't want to spook him; he might be the one to lead us to the bricks."

Ron nodded as he dialed a number through a burner phone. "Yo, boss said tail Pistol. But don't be seen," Ron said, then hung up.

The Yukon pulled off as I looked through the dark tint. Ever since I was kidnapped leaving the golf course, I've been on alert. Instead of two cars of shooters, now I have three. I always knew it, but Bishop reassured me: slippers count.

"Ron, keep the car running. I won't be long. I just want to see this nigga's reaction, and I'm out," I said as I grabbed my rain-stick cane and stepped out the car. Ron nodded as he stepped out the car to close my door for me.

"How can I help you, sir?" a guard at the front desk asked.

"I'm here to see my nephew, Kendrick Watson," I said as I pulled my state ID out of my wallet and slid it across the tall counter.

The female guard looked at her computer, then at my ID. I wasn't sure if I was on Kendrick's list, but I figured he would place me on there to make sure his T's were crossed, and his I's were dotted.

"Okay, sir. You're on his visiting list, but I'm seeing here that Mr. Watson has already received three visits for the week. And three is the max number for the week. I'm sorry, but you can try again next week," the lady kindly said.

I took my ID and placed it back in my wallet, then tucked the wallet into my back pocket. I pulled my money out. I wasn't sure how much it was, and I didn't care. I pulled the clip off the stack and slid it all across the counter, leaving my hand covering it.

The guard looked to me, then across her shoulder at a stocky Caucasian male guard. "I just want to see my nephew. He's not expecting me because I'm old. I'm sure this'll do for the inconvenience," I said then raised my hand.

The lady looked at the guard, then waved him over. She pulled the money from the counter, counted off a few hundred, and passed it to the male guard. "Can you escort this gentleman to the outside visiting area. And sir, your visitor will be with you shortly."

I nodded and placed my empty money clip into my pocket. I followed the male guard to my visiting area. I wasn't nervous, but my hands had begun to sweat. Kendrick wasn't just anyone. He was family. My nephew that I treated like my very own son. I taught him everything. He was my protégé. He was the next generation of me.

I wiped my hands on my pants as I sat at the picnic table outside. No matter what Kendrick was to me in the past, as of now, he was guilty of treason. And for that, he was my enemy.

Chapter 5

-Pistol-

As I pulled up to the block—and by the block, I mean Forest Lane, or as we call it, *The Lane*—I had to check in on my spot to make sure everything was everything. Once I was finished, I would take care of business for Ken.

The Lane wasn't just a street. It was my home away from home. I was originally from the *Stiff Cliff*—Oak Cliff, *Amerika* to be exact. I moved my hustle to North Dallas because the money just seemed to flow there. The Lane was more than just a street. It was the pathway to your dreams, especially if you're a dope boy. The known section of the Lane was Forest Lane and Audelia. That's the section Ken chose for his traps. It was a steady flow of hustlers, and youngstas that needed a steady supply. I chose the opposite end: Forest Lane and Abrams. My spot was Foresthill, right across the street from Wally World.

See, Ken had the most famous section in the Nawf, but my section was crack land. I was a real hustla. I knew times changed—that there was fentanyl and K2 changing the game. But one thing I knew: crack was still crack. Yeah, fentanyl was cheaper and the high was to die for, literally. But crack was authentic. It's been around since the early '90s, and yet it's 2025. What does that tell you?

I pulled around to the back of the apartments and parked, backing in to the gate. I stepped out and hit my alarm. This was my section, but that didn't stop the crackheads from stealing. I walked to the middle of the complex. It was a section of about twenty apartments, upstairs and downstairs. I rented four: two upstairs and two downstairs. The rent was cheap, considering it was a Section 8 complex. Being that it was, eighty percent of the people were down bad or addicts. Crack addicts.

Upstairs, I had the crack house on the left and the sherm on the right. Downstairs, I had the weed spot on the left and the coke house on the right. I sold fentanyl, too, but in a different section.

I didn't have a group of shooters standing around with their guns out like some gangsta movie. We didn't have to. We took care of our section and our people. There was nothing more loyal than a crackhead you treated with respect.

"Hey, Pistol," Seven shouted.

"Hey, Seven. How you doing?" I asked.

"I'm better now. Thank you for sending over some groceries," she said.

"It's no problem, Seven. You know we go way back," I assured her.

We gave her the name Seven when she became a crackhead back in the day. Before that, she was Courtney. Seven would only charge people seven dollars for sex. Back then, she was the only white woman on the block, so it was cheap even for a crackhead. In fact, Seven was the first crackhead I ever let suck my dick. She did it so good, I paid her ten dollars.

As I took the steps to go see the team, I could already hear where everyone was. MO3 was being played from our crack spot as loud as the speaker would allow. I pounded on the door with an open palm. Smurf, my son, answered the door with a Glock in his hand. He resembled his late mother in the face a little, but sadly, everything else he got from me. There was a lot I promised myself when Smurf was born. I promised myself I would always be in his life, and I promised myself I would protect him from the streets. I honestly felt the only way to protect him from the street life was to teach him the street life. It was the way my father taught me, and his father taught him. Some cycles work good when they don't change. Like the old saying: *If it ain't broke, don't break it.*

"Pops, what brings you to Mr. Rogers' Neighborhood?" Smurf asked.

I laughed as I walked past him into the apartment. Smurf was accompanied by his homies: Poppa, Trick-Trick, and Smurf's young protégé, Kidd. Poppa and Smurf grew up together. They both attended the same grade school, both playing for Lake Highlands High—that was until they chose the streets over the courts.

I'd met Trick-Trick when he moved to Dallas from Mississippi. All I knew back then was that Trick-Trick was on the run from the laws. Some people say he was a trapper; others say he was a shooter. If you ask around, the stories stay the same. One thing I can vouch for is if I need a shooter, he's the one to call. And if I front him some work, I always get paid.

Poppa—I've watched him grow up since he was a young teen. I can recall the first day I met him. I had to go to the school because Smurf and Poppa had jumped another kid for saying something about Poppa's deceased father. When I asked Smurf why he helped, he told me, "Pops, when an army moves in, they move as a unit. No man gets left behind." From that day forward, I treated Poppa as my own, and Smurf treated him as his blood brother.

I sat on the couch beside Kidd, who was weighing zips of crack. Trick-Trick was playing *Madden* against Poppa. There was two hundred dollars on the game console, so I knew they were gambling.

"What's good, Pops?" Poppa said. He had been calling me "Pops" for over ten years now.

"A lot. I can't lie. It's a lot," I said as I stared at the TV. It was the Cowboys against the Baltimore Ravens. I already knew who was playing with the Cowboys. It had to be Poppa, because Trick-Trick hated Dallas with a passion.

"What's the rundown?" I asked.

Poppa moved the game controller, pressing buttons as if he was in the game, spinning and juking himself. "Everything good so far. It's still early in the day, so, you know," Poppa said. He always used that phrase: *"You know."*

"Have you heard from Bull? He would usually hit me to re-up. I ain't heard from him in a few days."

Poppa shook his head without looking away from the screen. He was all into the game, and it had nothing to do with the money. What they were really playing for was bragging rights.

"Well, before the sun sets, you and Smurf pull up to his crib and see what's the deal. Check the county jail, see if he could've got jammed," I said. Poppa nodded again as if he heard me. "Overstood?" I said, making sure I was heard.

"You know, Pops, I gotcha," Poppa said, still jerking the controller left to right. "As soon as this game is over."

I laughed as I pulled out my cellphone. I remembered when me, Ken, and Squirrel used to chill together in our trap spot. We didn't have multiple spots like we do now; we used to sell everything in one spot. It was a one-stop shop. Hell, we even sold single cigarettes and condoms.

I scrolled down my contacts until I got to Squirrel's number. Ever since the night at the warehouse when Ken handed the throne to Angel, Squirrel's been MIA. I dialed his number. A woman's voice answered. I looked at the screen to see if I had dialed the right number.

"Hello?" the woman said. I shook my head. I had never known Squirrel to let a bitch answer his phone.

"I think I might have the wrong number," I said.

"Wait," the woman on the other end shouted. "The owner of this phone is in the hospital in critical condition. We've been trying to identify him, but he didn't come in with any identification. If you know this man, he's at Parkland Hospital. He needs his family. He needs prayer."

I hung up the phone. I looked at the screen, stunned.

"Pops, what's good?" Smurf asked, concerned.

First, my peoples—Big Ken—gets knocked by the Feds. Now Squirrel.

"I have to go. Y'all put the games down and take care of business," I shouted as I shoved my phone in my pocket and headed for the front door.

Chapter 6

-Ken-

I was called back down to visitation. I knew this had to be a record or something. I was just hoping for good news; I didn't know if my shoulders were strong enough for any more bad news. I went into the visitation room and was directed outside for an outdoor visit.

The sun was shining bright. It had been days since I was last out, so I had to cover my eyes with my hand to protect my vision. As I looked around, I saw a face I wasn't expecting to see. I walked up to the table and stood behind my uncle, Turtle. I stared at him. I knew he was up to something; he did everything like he was playing chess.

"You know it's rude to stand over people like that," Turtle said, feeling my presence. I walked around the table and sat across from him. We didn't hug or embrace. We never really did. Turtle rarely showed any emotion.

"Surprised to see me?" Turtle asked.

"Obviously. I mean, you weren't there at my trial. Not that I expected you to be, but each day I figured you'd pop up, even if you just sat in the back."

"You do recall I couldn't come to your trial? I was a little tied up." Turtle joked about his kidnapping like it was funny.

I hung my head. How soon I'd forgotten. "I hate that happened to you. I wish I could've done more."

Turtle laughed. "What could you have done, nephew?" he said. "I heard what the kidnappers requested. You didn't have a choice other than to send your wife."

I sighed as I thought about that day like it was yesterday. Bishop had me in the worst position I'd ever been in. I was forced to give in to his demands, all because I took his brother, Knight, out the game. That move cost me my queen.

"Unc', I wish I'd had more time to plan your rescue. To find another way so that . . . so that Angel didn't have to go out the way she did," I said.

"Yes, Angel . . . she went all out. She was the female version of you, for sure. My eyes were covered for the most part, but when she took the garment off my head, she had laid every—I mean, damn near everyone out. She died trying to untie me. Bitch nigga shot her in the back. She still stayed up long enough to turn around and kill the sucker," Turtle explained, before he began to cough.

Turtle looked down as he coughed into his fist. Something was off with him, and he knew I knew. He had taught me the game—which was his first mistake. *Never teach anyone your trades, especially if one day you plan to cross them.* That was Turtle's lesson to me.

"You sick, Unc'?" I asked as he stopped coughing. Turtle shook his head. "Nah, I just got this dry cough, is all," he said, wiping his mouth with the back of his hand.

I scooted closer and leaned over the table so he could hear me. "What happened to Angel's body, Unc'?" I asked just above a whisper.

"Nephew, when I tell you that I got out of there as fast as I could, that's exactly what I did. I was just happy to be alive. I stopped the first son of a bitch with a phone and called Ron to come and get me. Now that I think about it, I had no honor in how I handled Angel. I should've gone back for her. Luis called for a cleanup crew to dispose of the bodies."

"Do you think Luis has her body?" I asked, already knowing the answer.

"I went to see him, but I'm sorry, I didn't ask about her. I went to thank him for putting up the ticket to set me free, and I told him that I would pay him back for his loss."

"If everyone was killed, how did he take a loss? Did Angel not come through with the shipment?" I asked curiously.

Turtle laughed. "That Angel of yours only came through with a few ki's. No one knows where she stashed the others."

I looked at Turtle, puzzled. Now I knew why he'd sat across from me. He didn't have a hat on or a box of bait, but he was surely fishing.

"Damn," was all I said.

"Yeah, I know," Turtle added. "I wanted to get Luis something back. He had already lost two of his close comrades, plus the shipment. We've known each other for some time now, but business is still business."

I nodded. "Yeah. I overstand that," I said, just as alarms started blaring all around us. Guards began running in the same direction.

"Mr. Watson, I'm sorry, but we have to cut your visit short. We've been ordered to lock the unit down, immediately," a guard said to me.

I nodded and stood up. Turtle did the same.

"You have my number, if need be, call me," Turtle said as we shook hands and parted ways. I looked at my hand. I couldn't see it, but I could feel it. My hand felt slimy—the effects of touching a snake.

Chapter 7

-Pistol-

"How are you doing, ma'am? I'm—" I began to say, but I was cut off.

"Sign in first, sir," the nurse said, picking up the phone to answer a call. I shook my head and grabbed the clipboard. I signed my name under the visitors' list. I placed the clipboard on the counter, and waited for the nurse to finish her call.

"Okay, sir," she said as she hung up. She looked at the clipboard and asked, "Who are you here to see?"

"A friend. His name is Percy Jones," I said, calling Squirrel by his government name.

"Oh, I'm sorry. These hours are for family members only. You'll have to come at eight o'clock tomorrow," she explained.

"No, listen to me. I know y'all have rules here, but you have to understand—I *am* his family. At least all that he has that cares."

"What did you say his name was again?" she asked.

"Percy Jones," I said, hopeful.

"You're in fact his first visitor. He's in intensive care. I can allow you to see him, but I can only give you half an hour."

"Thank you."

"Room 37," she said as the phone rang again.

I walked down the hall, looking at every room on the way. When I made it to Squirrel's room, I noticed a chair outside the door with an empty *Dunkin'* coffee cup on the floor. If there was an officer here, he had given up his post for something else.

I walked inside the room. It was quiet besides the loud beeping hospital heart monitors. Squirrel lay in the hospital bed with a tube down his throat.

I stood over him and shook my head. It was crazy how just last week we were throwing a barbecue party for Ken, laughing and throwing back shots, reminiscing about how we got started. Looking at Squirrel, the joke was on us. Ken was given a life sentence, and Squirrel was fighting for his life.

I grabbed the bed rail. I wasn't on God's prayer list, and I wasn't going to beg for a favor I wouldn't to be able to repay back.

"Damn, Squirrel, homie. What happened to you, family?" I said more to myself, not sure he if could hear me.

"You not looking too good, family. So I'm wondering what the other nigga looks like. You need to snap back, family. We need you right now. The streets need you. I—"

I stopped when I heard footsteps behind me.

I turned to see a DPD officer eating a jumbo pretzel.

"Who are you?" the officer asked.

"I'm his brother, stepbrother," I said.

"Oh—" the officer said, sticking the pretzel in his mouth to shake my hand while he held a fresh cup of coffee in the other.

"It's sad to hear what happened to your brother. He's blessed to be amongst the living right now."

"What exactly happened, if you don't mind me asking?"

"Well, I wasn't one of the officers on the scene, but from what I was told, your brother was found in the trunk of a car. He'd been shot twice in the back."

I shook my head and sat down.

"But that's not it," the officer continued. "He wasn't alone."

I looked up, confused. “He wasn’t?”

“Nope. The driver was found on the scene, dead. As well as a lady—an Asian lady—who was found dead on the scene. Your brother was the lone survivor.”

I stood up, placing both hands behind my head as I began to pace. “I’m not understanding this. Who were the other victims?” I asked.

The officer shrugged as he bit into his pretzel. “No one knows. Neither of their bodies have been claimed,” the officer spoke with a mouthful.

“Damn. And no one has claimed the other two?”

“Yup. You were the first one to come forward. I can take you to the bodies and show you. If you can identify either one, then you’ll really help the investigation.”

My eyes lit up. I had to see who the other two were. “Yeah, I would like to see them.”

The officer drank from his coffee, then led the way. I hated leaving Squirrel unprotected, but I figured whomever shot him thought for sure they’d killed him, or else they wouldn’t have left him in the trunk.

“Debra, I have someone here to try to identify the two John Hancocks that came in the other night.”

“*John Hancock* is a signature, just so you know, Officer,” Debra said as she pulled out a dead body from the cold fridge, then another.

“Well, you knew what I meant,” the officer said, setting his coffee down and sticking the pretzel in his mouth as he unzipped the first body.

I looked at the Asian woman’s face. She was a complete stranger to me. I looked at the officer and shook my head. He went over to the next body and unzipped the zipper. I had to walk around him to see the person’s face. I had to do a double-take.

“Do you know him?” the officer said, holding the pretzel with the same hand he’d just unzipped the bag with.

I stared at Bull. He looked younger dead. He looked innocent—harmless compared to the killer the streets knew him as.

"Do you?" the officer asked again.

I shook my head. "I don't. Sorry."

I stared longer as the officer zipped Bull's lifeless body back up. Everything was in the box, but I still couldn't put all the pieces together. The officer said Squirrel was found in the trunk, so that only meant that Bull had to be the driver. Bull shot Squirrel. But why?

I shook my head. I didn't want to think it. The last conversation Ken and Squirrel had wasn't the best one. And everyone knew Bull was Ken's little man. Ken had been training Bull since Bull was in middle school.

I shook my head again. I didn't want to believe it, but the way it looked, Ken had thrown a rock at a glass house and tried to hide his hand.

Chapter 8

-Angel-

"Can you please change this shit?" I yelled at my babysitter. The TV had been on *ESPN* all damn day.

"What else is there to watch?" he said, grabbing the remote that was beside him on the couch.

"If you're not going to change it, then can you turn it down? Or off, hell," I said, annoyed.

He laughed as he turned the TV off and yawned. He stretched and kicked his feet up as if he was about to go to sleep.

"Un-uh. What you doing? You not about to go to sleep on me. A bitch already going to die. At least you can keep a bitch company."

My captor placed his hands behind his head to make himself more comfortable. "You don't have to die, Angel. All you have to do is give up the location of the bricks."

I laughed out loud. "Nigga, please. You think it's that simple, huh? '*Angel, you don't have to die. All you have to do is give up the location for the bricks*'," I mimicked him. "And then what? Sit here in these nasty panties until when? Turtle knows better. He knows he has to kill me."

"Why he have to kill you?" he asked.

"Because he knows if I ever get out of here, I will kill him."

He laughed at my statement.

"What's so funny?" I asked.

"You. Do you hear yourself? You really think you're a shooter? You really think you're a killer?"

"And you think I'm not?" I countered.

"I think you know how to use your pistol, but I'm not saying that makes you a killer. Now Ron—he's a killer. He has no heart; he has no emotions."

"Is that supposed to be a scare tactic? Good cop, bad cop shit?" I laughed.

"It's not a tactic. And I'm not trying to scare you. But you should be. As you said, Turtle knows better than to let you go. So that means only one thing, and that's that you're going to die. Unless you can convince him to keep you alive."

"And how do you suggest I do that?" I asked.

"Give him what he wants. But make him realize that you're worth more than those kilos. Make him remember how you put your life on the line to save him. And after all that, if he still intends to kill you, then he's not the leader I thought he was."

"While you're realizing he wasn't the man you thought he was, I'll be a dead bitch tied butt-naked to a tree with a pile of shit behind me," I said, still thinking about the gruesome story Ron put into my head.

"Naked, tied to a tree? What are you talking about?" he asked, confused.

"Nothing. It was just—nothing," I said, then looked at the man lying on the couch across from me. "Why are you so confident in Turtle? He's not the man you think he is."

"That's easy to say, yet you married a man who was taught everything by him."

"You don't know my husband, so don't start," I said, shocked that I was still defending him after all he did to me—after all I did to him.

"I know your husband better than you think I do," he said.

"Sure you do. What? You saw him in the streets or heard some rumors about him, and now you think you know my husband?"

The man sat up straight on the couch and looked at me. "My name is Nico Wright. Not sure if you know me, but me and your husband were best friends since grade school. We were literally each other's shadow. I had his back, and he had mine."

"If what you're saying is true, then why haven't I heard of you? Your name never came out of my husband's mouth. Ever."

"I guess he never speaks of me because I remind him of the worst part of his life," Nico said, then lowered his head as if he was reliving a dark part of his past.

"The worst part of his life? I doubt that. This has to be the worst part of his life. Oh, well, he spoke of losing a son once, but other than that, I doubt what you're saying is true."

"I was the reason he lost his son," Nico said sadly.

"How did you have anything to do with him losing his son? From what I was told, Lluvia got kidnapped, and that's how she lost her baby. That had nothing to do with you," I said, confused.

"I was the reason Lluvia got kidnapped. They were after me for some shit I did, so they came after me and everyone I loved," he said.

"If they wanted to kill everyone you loved, then why did they go after her? She was Ken's girl."

"Yeah, I guess you can say that. But at one point and time, she was mine. It . . . it's a long story," he said, leaving me on the edge of my seat, wanting more.

"No, no. You have to tell me. Because Ken never told me that he took her from his best friend."

"He didn't tell you because *I* took her from my best friend."

Chapter 9

-Ken-

I walked back into my cell. The cell had been tossed by the officers. It looked like a tornado had passed through. I looked at Slim.

"What the hell happened? I was only away for like twenty minutes."

"When they called you out for visit, we was all just chilling, and then Los said he felt like you were a law," Slim explained.

"Me?" I said, pointing at myself. "A law? Like twelve? The police?" I laughed.

Slim laughed as well. "He said that the only reason they kept calling you out was because you were talking to the DA. No one has that many visits back-to-back," Slim said, repeating what Los's words.

"So where's Los at now?" I said, looking around, ready to do whatever it took to clear my name. This was my first time being locked up, but if the rules were the same like the streets, you took care of whoever tossed dirt on your name, especially when being labeled a rat.

"He's gone. Blip smashed him for throwing your name through the mud. The law caught them fighting and locked them both up in segregation."

"So why the cell look like this?" I asked, picking up my bedspread from the floor.

"The law said Los told them we had a cell phone in here. So they tore the place up looking for it," Slim said, shaking his head.

"Crazy. A snitch calling someone a rat. The world has changed, huh," I said, then thought about something.

"Did they find the phone?" I asked, hoping they hadn't.

Slim shook his head. "Them laws too slow. I beat them every time. Why? You need it?" Slim asked, as he pulled out the small phone.

"Yeah, when you feel like it's a good time. I really need to send word to my peoples about the visit I just had."

"Who came to see you this time?" Slim asked, handing me the phone.

"My uncle, Turtle," I said, dialing Pistol's number.

"The infamous Turtle? Damn, I never thought he would come here," Slim said, sounding all excited.

"Me neither," I said, waiting for Pistol to answer.

"Ken," Pistol shouted into the phone as soon as he picked up. He was so loud I had to pull the phone away from my ear.

"What's up? What's got you all so excited?" I asked.

"It's Squirrel," was all he said.

"What you mean? What's up with 'im?" I asked, concerned.

"Man, it's a long story, so I'll give you the shortest version. He's in the hospital, bruh. He was shot. The police found him in the trunk of a car," Pistol explained.

"Shot? And they found him in the trunk of a car?"

"That's not all. Bull was driving the whip. They found him dead in the passenger seat, with an Asian woman also dead at the scene."

"Bull? My young man, Bull?" I asked to be sure.

"Yeah, family. That Bull."

I shook my head as I began to pace. It felt like the ground under me was crumbling. The world was exploding all around me. "I'm not understanding this. How did Bull end up dead, and who the fuck was the Asian woman? Nothing is making sense, Pistol," I said, looking up at the TV.

Pistol continued to talk, but his words were drowned out by what was being displayed across the screen.

"Ken. Do you hear me?" Pistol shouted.

"My bad, family," I said, still staring at the TV.

"What's the deal? What's going on?" Pistol asked.

"It's my lawyer."

"Your lawyer? What about your lawyer?" Pistol asked.

"He—he's on TV."

Chapter 10

-Emmanuel-

"You ready?" I asked Janice. We were at my house—well, I'm not sure it can be called a home anymore. We were here, packing as much as we could. Janice was moving to Oregon with her family, and she wanted me to tag along.

After I'd paid Kendrick a visit and told him my involvement in his demise, I wanted to do the right thing. I wanted to go to the District Attorney and explain what had transpired, but I couldn't. I wasn't made for prison. I was made for expensive Gators, thousand-dollar suits, and satin sheets. I'm a pretty boy, and everyone knows what happens to the pretty boy in prison.

"You sure this is all you need? Because once we leave this time, I never want to see this place again," Janice said, looking at the floor where the blood-stained carpet used to be.

We were in agreement; I didn't want to look back either. But first, I had to do one thing. "Wait here. I'll be right back," I said as I headed up the stairs.

When me and Hannah first bought the house, we had a lot of plans. We wanted a movie room, which we ended up finishing. We wanted a room for our workouts and a room for me, which was my office. Then there was the only empty room in the house: the one we had saved for a baby.

I walked into the bedroom—the room where all the memories were. The good and the bad ones. I'd appreciate them all the same, I was sure. I do wonder at times where my life would be if she hadn't cheated. If I'd actually come home on our anniversary and she had been waiting for me . . . waiting to be held and loved. But life doesn't have a rewind button. The woman I loved was gone. So the house we bought together? It wasn't a home.

I wiped tears away as I walked back down the stairs. *I'm ready now.*

Janice looked through the peephole with her hand on the doorknob. Since the incident, we always checked the peephole first. "We got a problem. A big problem," she said, looking back at me.

"What is it?" I asked, hoping it wasn't more of Angel's goons coming to finish the job.

"There's people out there," she said.

"People? What people?"

"News people and police."

I walked to the window and pulled the blind down just a tad. There were police and several news vans parked all over. Even a small crowd of my neighbors was huddled in the background.

". . . We are here reporting live for Fox News, where the SWAT team is preparing to apprehend a suspected killer whom everyone knows as Emmanuel Stevens, one of the most prominent lawyers in all of Texas."

I looked over my shoulder at the mention of my name. Janice had turned the television on, and my face was plastered across it with a live feed of the action outside my house. I looked at Janice; she looked at me.

"What are we supposed to do?" she asked.

"We aren't going to do anything," I said, walking back to the window. I could now hear police screaming through a bullhorn.

"What are you talking about? We have to do something or else they'll come in," Janice said.

"You're going to go out first. Tell them you're my lawyer and that I'm going to turn myself in."

Janice shook her head as tears began to fall from her eyes. "This wasn't how it was supposed to be."

I walked up to her and wrapped my arms around her. I kissed her forehead, then the top of her head. "Shh—now's not the time for tears. This is your time to shine. Go out there and command their attention. I need you to be strong, because in order to get out of this mess, we're going to need it."

Janice looked up at me and kissed me passionately. I grabbed her around the waist and cupped her soft ass. As she pulled away, she wiped her tears and walked up the stairs. Minutes later, she emerged wearing a pencil skirt and a button-down shirt with matching heels. Looking closely, I noticed the outfit came from Hannah's closet.

Janice walked right by me with her phone in one hand and the matching suit jacket in the other. She walked to the door and put the jacket on. She took a deep breath and unlocked the lock. She opened it slightly and waved her hand outside.

I looked at the TV. You could see her hand vividly on camera. Members of the SWAT team began to spread out with their guns drawn at the front door. Camera crews began to move closer despite officers' demands to stay distant. Janice walked out the door with her hands held high. She walked slowly toward the police.

"Ma'am, were you held hostage?" a news reporter asked.

Janice shook her head. "My client, Emmanuel Stevens, is innocent until proven guilty. Unknowingly, my client has been charged with a series of crimes that we will fight in a court of law to prove false. My client will come out only when he is guaranteed he will not be harmed," Janice spoke confidently.

Reporters began to ask questions one after the other. Janice held up her hand, silencing them all. "Like I said, once I get a call from the Chief of Police telling me personally my client will not be harmed, my client will turn himself over to the authorities. And with me there, he will answer any questions he sees fit to answer."

I smiled as I watched Janice put on a show. She held her ground in a way that I would. Janice looked down at her phone. She answered it and nodded. She looked into the camera and said, "The Chief of Police has confirmed my client will not be harmed. He will now turn himself in to start the process of proving his innocence."

I took her words as my cue. I opened the door wide. My hands were raised high above my head. The sun beat down, turning the sidewalk into an oven, but the real heat was coming from the red laser dots dancing across my chest. SWAT members and DPD's finest had their automatic weapons trained on my life, their fingers itching for me to give them a reason.

I dropped to my knees, feeling the grit of the concrete bite into my slacks–thousand-dollar fabric meeting a ten-cent sidewalk. I laced my fingers behind my head, and before I could even draw a clean breath, they stormed me.

It was a blur of heavy boots and Kevlar. Rough hands snatched my arms, nearly wrenching them out of their sockets, while another officer hiked up my silk shirt to check my waistband for steel. They hauled me to my feet, the zip-ties biting deep into my wrists. As the lead officer started rattling off the Miranda rights, I just nodded. I didn't need the lecture. I'd spent my whole career telling men how to shut up; now, it was finally my turn.

Chapter 11

-Turtle-

The surprise visit with Ken didn't go as planned. He sat across from me, within arms reach. I had him right where I wanted him, and yet it wasn't good enough. I had taught Ken the game. I showed him how to move and how to evade. He proved he had been listening, because the bait I tossed at him came back with only half a worm. He'd gotten close enough to the edge to see me. He nibbled on the bait without shaking the line, and here I was, sitting there looking like a laughingstock.

But I had a trick for him. See, after years of using worms for so long, you have to switch it up. It was time for some different bait.

"Angel, Angel, Angel," I taunted, speaking her name as I walked into the room where she was being held captive.

Nico jumped up from where he had been lying on the couch. Angel turned her attention from the TV to me as I walked in, my cane making a heavy *thud* with each step I took.

"Is everything okay, OG?" Nico asked as he stood

A smirk crept onto my face. A plan had formed in my head by pure chance. "Yeah, everything is just fine. I—I was just coming to let Angel know that I just visited with her husband. He's looking . . . I guess you could say he's just looking. He's worried about you. I told him you were killed in the fiasco. So I figure when I go back to see him he'll be looking, a bit different."

Angel didn't bother to say a word. She just stared at me, pure hatred steaming from her eyes. I could feel hers, and I wondered if she could feel mine.

"Nico, a word," I said, turning to leave.

Nico walked behind me, closing the door. I walked into my office and took a seat in my large leather chair.

"Is everything okay?" Nico asked again.

I nodded slowly as I grabbed my vintage cognac decanter and two glasses. I poured the cognac and handed one to Nico.

"Everything is perfect, Nico. And with your help, it's going to get better." I raised my glass to his.

Nico touched his glass to mine, and we downed the liquor, feeling it burn all the way down.

"Anything I can do to help, and it's done," Nico said.

"I want you to do something for me. And it's not going to be too hard, because you've done it in the past."

"Okay, and what's that?" he asked.

"I need you to make Angel trust you. Make her fall in love with you."

"You want me to take Angel from Ken?" he asked.

"Exactly. Just like you did with Lluvia in the past," I said, smiling.

Nico sat quiet, as if he was debating my demand.

"Nico, this wasn't a proposition. I need you to get her to trust you. Get her to depend on you—just enough to where she'll show you where the bricks are."

"Turtle . . . she won't trust me. She knows I'm loyal to you."

I smiled as I pointed my finger at him. "You're right. She knows you're loyal to me. But when you do this, she'll think otherwise."

"Do what, exactly?" he asked.

"Help her escape."

Chapter 12

-Angel-

I hated his old ass. My mama used to tell me, *everything slick don't slide*. And his old ass swore up and down he was the slickest there ever was. But wasn't anything sliding past me without me noticing.

He came in telling me that he went to see Ken, like I gave two fucks. I didn't give a shit—hell, I was the one that put him there. Then he takes Nico out for a private whisper. If he was so damn gangsta, why didn't he say the shit in front of me? I didn't care, nonetheless, because I was working on a plan of my own. One that would get me the hell out of this damn chair, for starters.

As I was wiggling in the chair, doing my best to loosen the straps that kept me held hostage, Nico opened the door, causing me to stop. Nico took the seat he'd just left vacant and placed his hands over his face. He shot to his feet just as fast as he sat down and began to pace.

"Nico, what the hell is wrong with you?" I had to ask. His ass was making me nervous.

"It's Turtle," he said as he paced. "He's losing his damn mind. At first, he kidnapped you to scare you into telling him where you stashed the bricks. Now he says to hell with the bricks; he just wants to kill you."

I smiled. "Boy—stop." I laughed. "That's the best you got? You come in here acting like a bitch about to die, thinking that'll scare me? You got to try a little harder, lil' daddy."

Nico pulled a pocketknife from his pocket and walked up to me. Me and my fat mouth—I'd finally bitten off more than I could chew. But if I was going out, a bitch wasn't going out pleading. *Naw, naw.* I was going out the same way I came in: talking shit.

"Fuck you, nigga. You just like a bitch, stabbing me in the back. Kill me face-to-face," I shouted as Nico walked behind me with the knife in his hand. "Bitch-ass nigga, I'ma haunt you forever—"

I stopped when I felt my restraints cut from my wrists. I looked over my shoulder as Nico folded the knife and placed it back in his pocket.

"Put those pants on and make it quick. We have to hurry before Turtle gets done taking a shit."

I stood up and looked down at the chair I'd been tied to for the past week. "Nico, what the fuck is going on?" I asked as I stepped into the pants that were on the floor. They were mine, and they smelled like piss.

"I'm getting you out of here," was all he said as he checked the safety on his pistol.

"What—?" I started to say.

Nico held his hand up, silencing me. "If you want to stand here and talk, then I'll just tie yo' lil' ass back up to the chair," he said, looking at me. "That's what I thought," he added once I didn't utter a word.

If Nico was really going to help me escape, I wasn't going to stop him.

"You ready?" Nico asked.

Nico opened the door, and when he did, Turtle stood on the opposite side by his lonesome. I knew this was too good to be true. I just knew it.

"Nico, what is this?" Turtle asked as we all stood in shock.

Nico placed his left hand on my side, pulling me directly behind him as if he were protecting me. I looked at his back, wondering what had gotten into him.

"I can't let you go through with this, Turtle. This ain't what I signed up for," Nico said as he pulled his gun and aimed it at Turtle.

"You can't let me do this? Do what—kill a bitch that had every intention of killing me? You done got a soft spot for this little demon, huh?" Turtle shouted.

Ron heard the shouting and walked into the room like he'd just woken up from a nap. Noticing the gun aimed at Turtle, Ron drew his Glock and aimed it at Nico.

Turtle saw where things were headed. "Ron, lower your weapon."

Ron shook his head. "Can't do it. This faggot is a traitor, and he gots to die," Ron said, gripping his Glock tighter.

"I don't want to shoot you, Turtle. But I'm not dying here, and neither is she," Nico said, waving his pistol from Turtle to Ron.

"Nobody is going to die. Ron, put your gun down, now," Turtle shouted.

"Turtle—" Ron began to say.

"Now," Turtle demanded.

Ron huffed as he leaned down and placed his gun on the ground. I took that as my cue to pick the gun up.

"Leave it!" Nico said as I went for the weapon.

"We have to kill them, or they'll find us and kill us," I said.

"Nah, Turtle won't come after us," Nico said, seeming so sure of himself. "I am my father's son, Turtle. So if you do come after me, I will pull the trigger next time," Nico promised.

"You're going to have to, soft-ass nigga. You just like yo' daddy. Always soft on women. Look at you—you got a thing for Ken's women, huh? You just want to be like him so bad, you just couldn't help yourself," Turtle taunted.

I could see the anger rising on Nico's face. He was doing his best to contain it, but Turtle didn't stop talking. Nico reared back with the butt of his pistol and smashed it across Turtle's head.

"Mother—" Ron shouted as Turtle fell to the ground. Blood seeped from the gash on the side of his head.

Nico huffed as he pointed his pistol at Ron. Ron looked as if he wanted to jump stupid, like he was bulletproof or something. Turtle held his hand up, stopping Ron from losing his life trying to prove his loyalty.

"Let them go," Turtle said, looking up at Nico and me from the floor.

Nico grabbed my hand as he stepped over Turtle with his pistol aimed at Ron. As bad as I wanted to smile, I didn't. I was free? I knew Nico setting me free came at a price. And I knew it would be steep.

Chapter 13

-Emmanuel-

I felt like shit—like a bum on the street watching the world pass me by. I was the guy people saw, but no one stopped to say hello. I had been sitting in an interrogation room for almost three hours, and no one had even peeped their head into the room to even see if I had to pee.

But, being a defense attorney, I knew their tactics. They wanted me to get fidgety in my seat while they watched from behind the camera. They wanted me to get upset at being kept waiting. They wanted me to beat on the door so they could come in like they had forgotten I was in the room—only to apologize and ask if I needed anything to drink, or to see if maybe I wanted a smoke.

I knew every room they were going to make. The playbook they used was the original one; the playbook never changed. Only the good cop and the bad cop. I knew it would be another ten or twenty minutes before they come in to question me. Or maybe they knew of me—the top lawyer in the city. Maybe they were calling an audible. But even then, it would be from a play they'd once used.

"Mr. Stevens, sorry to have kept you waiting," an older, Hispanic detective said, entering the room. Behind him was another detective, a little younger with a mustache. I already knew which was which. It was obvious.

They both took their seats across from me. The older one took a drink from his brown coffee cup and smiled at me from across the table. I looked at him, confused. This was a murder investigation; I didn't see what was so funny.

"Mr. Stevens, you're not new to the system, so you should know how this is going to go. To help us all save some time, you can help us by being honest. We can get the ball rolling so we can all put this behind us."

I remained silent.

"Okay, you don't have to talk, but if you would just listen to me for a minute," the older detective said. "We found your wife dead with a male who people claim they never saw her with. They were in a truck registered to you. And in the bed of your truck was a dead body. His body was wrapped in a rug—a rug we think came from your home. Now, Mr. Stevens, if we were to check your home, do you think we'll find traces of their blood or fabrics from the same rug?"

I remained motionless and silent. The other detective huffed and stood to his feet. He grabbed the file from the table, held it up, then slammed it down. The contents spread out in front of me.

"I hate people like you—thinking you're smarter because you had a privileged life, walking around in your fancy suits. You killed those people, and you thought you were going to get away with it. Your neighbor gave a statement about you being naked in your driveway a few weeks ago; you had a gun. So, what happened? You found your wife out with another man? She got tired of you being a lousy fuck? Working all those long hours? She wanted a real man, huh? You were too embarrassed to let her go, so you followed her and then you killed them, huh? And the one in the trunk—he was just an innocent witness, so you killed him, too? Is that how it went?"

He continued to rant. He pulled photos of the crime scene out and tossed them at me. Pictures of Hannah laid out on the concrete—dead, lifeless. I did my best to look away, but I couldn't help myself.

Images of the woman I'd always loved lay in front of me. The one I knew to always be happy, cheerful. Yet, she wasn't smiling now. I was supposed to love, honor, and cherish her. She was my wife, despite our differences. She wasn't supposed to be dead. She was innocent. She was the real innocent witness who was murdered.

So the detective is actually wrong on that the allegation that I murdered wife. But he isn't wrong about the reality of it. In a way, he is right. I am not the one who pulled the trigger, but in a way—I am the one who killed her. If only I'd worked less and been a husband more, Hannah would still be alive. The baby in her stomach would still be alive. My silence isn't just a legal strategy anymore; it's the weight of everything I'm losing in real-time.

I tried to keep my composure, tightening every muscle in my face to keep the mask from slipping. *Show no emotion. Remain silent. Don't give these bastards a single drop.* I was doing good at first, but the more I looked at Hannah's pictures, the harder it got. My eyes were glued to the photos, pinned there by the sight of the woman who used to be my peace. I was paralyzed in grief for her and our unborn child. Tears began to fall—more like a river. Pain was released; regret was pouring out.

"Okay," I said through sobs. "Okay, I'll tell you everything!"

The detectives both smiled. Then the door opened, and in walked Janice in a new business suit, power flowing from her.

"No, you won't. My client has the right to remain silent, and that's exactly what he'll do," Janice said, crossing her arms.

I wiped my tears as I looked at her. She had perfect timing.

Chapter 14

-Nico-

The game was fucked up. And the OGs compare it to the game of chess, and Turtle was playing the game to his advantage. Sadly, I was just a pawn in it all—the one that was always sacrificed for the cause, like I wasn't worth shit. But what if I made it to the other side? I would come out more important than anyone else. So, I was down to play the game, but with a different set of rules.

I drove through Dallas with my mind heavy. Angel sat in the passenger seat, but at the moment, I paid her no mind. My mind was on what Turtle said to me only minutes ago. He said I was just like my pops, soft on women. He even had the nerve to say I wanted to be like Ken. I know we were supposed to make it all look convincing, but I'd got in my feelings. His accusations struck a nerve. It was bad enough that's how the streets saw me: the guy who stole his day-one's girl. My father had done the same thing back in the day to his own day-one, and it shamed him the same way it shamed me.

I was never forgiven for what I did. Even though I never asked for forgiveness, I figured Ken would've forgiven me—at least for his sake. I knew once he heard about this, he would hate me forever. Then I remembered that Angel was supposed to be dead.

I looked out the corner of my eye to Angel. She was bobbing her head to Lil Wayne's *Tha Carter VI* album. The song "Sharks" was playing. It was one of my favorite songs from the album, and it seemed like it was her favorite, too, as she recited the lyrics word for word:

Snakes ain't always in the grass. Sharks ain't always in the water. Thieves ain't always in the night. God ain't always at the altar. I learned to live with one eye open. Takes getting bit a couple times to know that snakes ain't always in the grass. Sharks ain't always in the water.

I turned the radio down a tad. "What you know about that?" I asked. I didn't look at her, keeping my eyes on the road. But I could feel her eyes on me.

"What? The song, or real-life shit?" she asked.

"Both."

"The song is one of the deepest Wayne has ever recorded. But when I listen to it, I imagine my life," she said.

"So what was it? The shark or the snake that bit you?"

"Both," she said. "But it wasn't those that hurt the most."

"What you mean?" I asked.

"The thieves. They were something else. Big Ken . . ." She sighed. "He was the worst thief I've ever encountered. He stole my heart right in front of me without even noticing it. He was a professional."

"But even then, I know that didn't faze you. You got bit by snake niggas and sharks. Him stealing your heart couldn't have fazed you that much. I can see you're stronger than that."

"I wasn't torn, if that's what you mean. I was hurt that he didn't take care of my heart when he had it. But that didn't break me; that was what drove me," she explained.

"So, what broke you?"

"God. He really wasn't at the altar," she said.

I looked her way. I didn't know what to say, or if I was supposed to say anything at all. I understood her pain. I too had been bit by sharks and snakes. I'd had my heart stolen, too—just so happened it was by my day-one's girlfriend. And I could relate to God not being at the altar. Many nights I called on Him and never got an answer.

I pulled up to my hideaway and parked.

"You brought me to your home? Turtle will find us here. We can't stay here," Angel said.

I turned the radio off. "This isn't my home. It's more like a safe house. No one that knows me has been here. You're the first. I promise," I assured her.

She nodded and opened the car door. I pulled a key from my glove compartment and handed it to her.

"You're not coming?" she asked, sounding concerned.

"I have to go get food. I'm not normally here, so everything is probably spoiled. Don't worry, I'll be okay." I smiled.

"I wasn't worried, trust," she pretended. I laughed. "Just hurry back," she added.

I nodded as she got out of the car. I waited until she walked into the house, then drove off. I said I wouldn't put myself in this predicament ever again. The last time was just too . . . too humiliating. But I guess Ken just had great taste in women. Or why else would I be falling for yet another one?

Chapter 15

-Turtle-

A glass of cognac temporarily soothed the throb that came from my forehead. I placed the glass to the side of my head, hoping the ice inside would soothe the burn.

"Damn, Boss, I still can't believe Nico smacked you upside your head with his gun," Ron said as he grabbed my glass to refill it.

"I told you, he did what he had to do to make it all look real. Or else Angel would've known. It was all necessary in my book," I assured him.

Ron handed me a glass of cognac as he sat down across from me. "But what if she still don't trust him? What if she never tells him where the ki's are? What's our next stop, then?" Ron asked a good question. One I hadn't asked myself.

"What if Angel turns him against you? What if he jumps ship and ride for her? All those ki's she has . . . that's more than enough to buy someone's loyalty," Ron continued.

I sat and thought about what Ron said. Angel was a beautiful woman. And a hundred ki's could turn even the most loyal comrades. Nico had his flaws. He did turn his back on his best friend for a piece of pussy. But he was younger then. Just a kid. He could've grown up, learned from his mistakes. Left the past in the past. Matured, maybe. I wasn't sure, so I didn't answer Ron. I only hoped.

"Cat got your tongue, unc'?" a voice said, startling me and Ron, catching us by complete surprise. Nico walked in the room with a grin on his face. The bulge of his gun was evident on his hip. Nico walked to the bar and grabbed himself a glass. he placed two ice cubes in it and poured himself a measure of my most expensive taste on the shelf. As Nico took a sip, he savored the flavor. His eyes closed as he enjoyed the exquisite taste. That was the side effect of drinking Armand de Brignac. Considering it cost me three hundred large a bottle, it was only right it made him feel that way.

I waited until Nico took his seat before I responded to his question. Instead of sitting with us, he chose to sit at the bar, overlooking us. I paid it no mind, but I could see it got to Ron.

"Unc', you assigned me with a task, and now you don't think I can complete it?" Nico asked.

"Don't jump to conclusions, Neph'. Ron was just trying to figure out our plan. What would be plan B if plan A was to fail?"

"If plan A was to fail? Nico said as he took a swig from his glass, then stood up. "Plan A will work. Because it has to work. We don't have any other options. The only question is, when she tells me where they are, how many can I keep?"

"I knew it," Ron shouted as he jumped to his feet in a rage. "I knew you had an ulterior motive. You only did what you did to get something, not out of loyalty."

"What are you saying?" Nico countered.

"I'm saying you took Angel for leverage, not because it was asked of you. I know your type, and I've always been on point," Ron said.

"What's my type then, huh?"

"Just because your scales aren't showing doesn't mean you don't still hiss when you talk," Ron said.

"Nigga, who are you calling a snake," Nico said, getting defensive.

"Both of you, calm the fuck down. This isn't the time, nor the place, to shout your differences. We got a common enemy, so for now, that makes us friends. Okay?" I said, hoping they could let their differences go for the common goal.

"Unc', despite what you may be thinking, we have the same plan. We share the same goal. I want to help you get the ki's. I want to help you get revenge. I just wanted to know the plan after the success. Where do I come in after you're back on the throne?"

"Neph', the plan has always been to take care of my right hand and my left hand," I emphasized, gesturing toward Nico and Ron. "But we have to get those kilos from Angel. We have to."

"I'ma do my part, Unc'. I'ma take care of business. I'll get her to talk to me. To open up and trust me enough to take me to the ki's."

"How can you be so sure?" Ron asked.

"Because—" Nico answered, irritated by Ron's question. "Because I could tell by how she looks at me. She wants someone she can confide in. She wants to be able to truly trust someone. And I think she wants to be able to get back at you, Turtle. She's not going to let it go that you kidnapped her. And she knows none of Ken's soldiers will ever come after you; therefore, she'll keep me around. The guy who hit you across the head with a pistol," Nico explained.

He actually made a good point. But I still had a question of my own. "Why'd you leave her at your place alone?" I asked.

"I felt I had to. You kidnapped her, held her against her will. I rescued her. Me leaving her alone showed her I wasn't doing it for an ulterior motive."

"So, let me ask you this. If you were kidnapped and held against your will, then rescued and left alone at your rescuer's home, would you stick around or leave at the first opportunity you had?" I asked, hoping he would catch on.

"Shit," Nico shouted as he stormed for the front door. I laughed and shook my head.

"Do you think he'll get the job done, or were you just hoping he could?" Ron asked.

"After talking to him, I think he can. But I hope Angel is still there."

"Why would he leave her alone? I still don't understand that theory," Ron said as he grabbed the bottle of Armand de Brignac and poured us both a glass.

"She won't go far if she was to leave. There aren't many roads where she's at," I pointed out.

"How you know? I don't even know where Nico lives," Ron said as he handed me my glass.

"I used to smash the realtor that sold him the place. So even though he thinks it's a safe house, it's far from it," I smiled.

"You sly devil." Ron smiled as he touched his glass to mine.

"Like you said, sometimes you can't see the scales."

Chapter 16

-Nico-

I did the dash, racing to my place to see if Angel had ghosted me. I was praying she'd stuck around. If she'd ghosted me, I would definitely be the laughingstock of the team.

As I pulled up, I killed the engine and stepped out of the car, slamming the door behind me. There was no point in locking the doors; my place was in Lancaster, far out on the dirt roads, meaning my neighbors were acres away.

Making it to the front door, I reached in my pocket for the key. As I began to place it in the lock, I noticed the door was partially open. Off instinct, I pulled out my Glock. I pushed the door open slowly. A few situations began to play in my head. It wasn't likely—since no one knew where I lived—yet I still felt that maybe somehow Turtle had sent someone to capture Angel and take her back, thinking I wasn't capable of completing the job.

Then another thought came to mind, one that would surely embarrass me in front of my peers: Angel had left as soon as I'd driven away. She'd left and hadn't even bothered to fully close my door, trekking down the road until someone finally pulled over and gave her a ride.

Quietly easing into the house, I closed the door behind me. I stood still, listening for a sound or any movement. I started for the living room; there was no sign of Angel or anyone else. I headed for the stairs, then checked the guest room. Again, nothing. The same for the guest bathroom. Nothing.

I headed toward my room. The door was ajar. I eased toward it with my gun drawn. Noise came from inside the bedroom. As I inched closer, I noticed it was from the stereo. I pushed the door open slowly with the tip of my gun.

"I know people say that I'm dangerous, but as you can see, I don't have a weapon," Angel joked. She was lying on my bed, completely naked.

I walked into the room and looked around, then my eyes landed on her—on her perfectly naked body.

"Angel, what are you doing? Where are your clothes?" I asked, unable to take my eyes off her as she lay so gracefully on my bed.

Angel rose to her knees, crawling across the mattress toward me. My eyes went to the curve of her backside. My body started to heat up in places I knew were out of my control—places that had betrayed me before.

Angel stood in front of me on her knees. Her small, yet perfect *twins* looked tasty. I bit my tongue lightly to keep it in my mouth.

"I'm not doing anything you haven't desired me to do, Nico. I'm going to be truly honest with you; after all you've done for me, I feel that you deserve honesty. At first, I thought about leaving. I even pictured the face you would make once you came back and saw that I was long gone. But I then thought about everything you've done for me—how you risked everything, how you put it all on the table to save me," Angel explained as she inched closer.

My mind was telling me to keep my distance. To stay in my own safe space. Social distance. But somehow, my legs were getting the wrong signal from my brain. My brain was saying to step away from the premises, yet my legs kept moving forward.

I stared into her eyes as the music read my thoughts. I'd heard the song before, but this time, Teddy Swims had me feeling like I'd written those lyrics myself.

Are you . . . Are you . . . Are you . . . Are you . . . Made up in my head or are you in my bedroom? Questions that I ask ever since I met you.

"Angel, I did what I did because I felt like you didn't deserve the treatment you received just for being loyal. I figured if Turtle would do you like that after you saved his life, then my loyalty to him was expiring, too. I pride myself on loyalty. I mean, I learned to."

"And that's why I decided to stay, Nico. If I was to leave, then I was no greater than him. I owe you more than that."

"So, you pay me by getting naked?" I asked.

"No. I took a shower, and I didn't have any clean clothes to put on. So, I just came to lie down. And as I was lying here, I couldn't help but think about what you had said about Turtle."

My mind began to race. She had lost me. *Did she overhear me and Turtle planning the whole thing?*

"What did I say? And Turtle?" I asked, trying not to sound concerned.

"You told me once that you took Lluvia from Ken, and as I was lying here, I couldn't help but wonder—how? Was it the way you handled business? Your swag, or your smile?" she said as she inched closer.

"I don't want to relive the past, or why Lluvia liked me," I said.

"Shh . . ." she hushed me, placing her finger over my lips. "I'm not trying to upset you, Nico. I'm just wondering what was the wedge that came between her and Ken? Because . . ." Angel said seductively as she reached for my jeans.

She unzipped the zipper and stuck her hand inside. She gripped my pipe through my boxer briefs and said, "I was wondering if *this* was the wedge that came between them. And could you use it to break us apart, too?"

I took a deep breath as she gripped my dick. Her hand was soft—a massage-like feeling to my strained, hard dick. But I had to stop her. I couldn't fall for her tricks. I just knew this was a trick. And even though I knew it was a setup, I couldn't keep my eyes off her treats.

"Angel, we shouldn't—" I began as she gripped me harder, her lips finding mine and taking my breath away.

As our kiss broke, Angel unbuttoned my jeans, then slid them and my boxers down in unison. My dick jumped, happy to be freed. Angel stood still in front of me; she eyed it with her mouth open.

"Now I see," she said. As she rubbed between her legs, using her own wetness, she stroked me with a tight grip.

My eyes went to the back of my head. My head leaned back as she stroked me up and down.

"Angel, stop. We have to . . . stop," I pleaded as the feeling began to take over.

"No, we don't. Let me show you my loyalty," she said as she crouched down to take me in her mouth.

I opened my eyes as I felt her breath on me. "No," I shouted as I jumped back and pulled up my clothes.

"Nico, don't. We both need this," Angel tried to persuade me.

As I looked at her naked body, I wanted nothing more than to dive on top of her and taste every inch, but I knew better. I knew the power of pussy—the way it could control a man, no matter how strong-minded he was, or thought he was.

And to make matters worse, Giveon was in the background singing about how it all felt like a dream. He had a point. Because when I first laid eyes on Angel, tied to that chair, I wondered what kind of woman she was. The time she asked me to pull her thong off, I couldn't help but wonder how she would feel on top of me, with me inside of her. But having her in front of me, it all felt like a dream—one I didn't want to wake up from, but one I had to wake up from.

"We just can't, Angel. We can't," I said over my shoulder as I walked out of the room.

In the hall, I placed my back against the wall. I couldn't believe I'd just turned down the most beautiful woman I'd ever seen.

Chapter 17

-Angel-

I couldn't believe this nigga. He really has the audacity to pass this tight pussy up, like he was trying to prove a point to himself or something. If he was, then he'd already failed. As soon as his dick got hard, he exposed his hand. I can't lie—I did want him. Probably more then he wanted me.

When I first saw him, I was tied to that chair. Even in my worst moment, I thought he was cute. When I tried to seduce him the first time, I felt that I almost had him. But being that at that moment I was still held hostage at the time, I sensed he wouldn't bite. But once he rescued me and saw me completely naked, I just knew he wanted me. Or at least I thought he did.

I laid back on Nico's bed. I closed my eyes and laughed to myself. I had never been turned down before. I guess there was a first time for everything.

I sighed as I crossed my legs. Just the thought of what I wanted him to do to my pussy still had me on fire. Crossing my legs didn't help none. It felt that I'd added gasoline to the fire.

I opened my legs, which was like someone opening a window in a house fire. I felt myself blowing up on the inside, like my whole body was engulfed in flames. I knew the only way to get the feeling to go away was to put the fire out myself, seeing the fireman wasn't interested.

Raising my left leg, I massaged the area around my clit. My body jerked at the feeling. My pussy was soaking wet.

Spreading my legs, I massaged my clit with my right hand as my left went to my hard nipples. My thoughts went to Ken, the man who normally would be the one putting my fire out. I thought about the way we made love the last time—how we went all night long. Then I began to think about Nico, wondering if he could use his dick the way Ken did, or if Nico's was just for show.

"*Umhhh.*"

Moans escaped my closed mouth as I tried to mask my pleasure. I kept my eyes shut as I envisioned Nico and Ken both staring at me, both of them stroking their long dicks while I pleasured myself. A competition among men—both of them doing their best not to cum first. Bodies jerking, fists closed tight as they both grunted, holding back their own moans of pleasure.

"Uhh, Ken," I moaned, massaging my clit faster. "Nico," I gasped as my eyes rolled into the back of my head.

I could feel myself on the edge, but I wasn't ready. It wasn't time. So I fought myself to stay. To keep going . . . at least for a little longer. But the pressure—the feeling of my body crashing, falling deep into complete bliss—it was all so tempting.

"Shit . . . Ken . . . Nico." I moaned their names, both of them taking turns on my pussy in my mind.

The bed under me jerked, bringing me out of my fantasy and back to reality. I opened my eyes to see Nico leaning over me, between my legs, completely naked. His dick was hard in his hand, lined up between my legs and aimed at my tight hole.

"You don't need him. I'm here now." His tongue tasted like Hennessy—*Courage Juice*, as I like to call it.

As we kissed, I could feel his dick bumping against my swollen clit. The softness of his mushroom head felt like a new cotton pillow, and I was ready to get put to bed. I wanted my mouth open with spit and drool everywhere.

"You sure you want to do this? You seemed unsure minutes ago," I asked as I lay back to get a good look at the sexy hunk of a man towering over me, his sword in hand, ready to slay his own dragon.

"I'll show you how sure I am," Nico said as he leaned down and sucked my tongue into his mouth.

I opened my eyes wider, our tongues doing the bump and grind. My legs opened voluntarily; my hand went between us. I grabbed his dick, feeling up and down his shaft. My eyes were closed, but if you were to put his dick in a lineup, I'd be able to point it out. The veins that crossed each other . . . I was getting impatient.

I guided his dick to my entrance. The head poked at my hole, my pussy juices pouring out of me. As our tongues danced, his dick finally hit home. The feeling was like one I'd never experienced before—like I was a virgin all over again. My body jerked and my back arched, but our lips never departed. I opened my eyes to see if I was feeling what I was feeling or if it was all a dream. I looked at Nico as he stroked my pussy the way pussy is supposed to be stroked. He didn't pound me hard and fast; he took his time, rotating his hips with each stroke.

"Ohh, Nico . . . Nico, baby . . . shit." I moaned as my pussy creamed. The sensation felt like more than just sex. It was like heaven. Like my body was floating. "Right there," I moaned, hoping he could keep this performance up all night.

Nico was doing a damn good job of not moaning, but I could tell that my sweet, juicy, tight pussy was getting to him—the way he was biting his lips, the way he kept closing his eyes. Yeah, my shit was the bomb.

"*Unhh—*" Nico held back his words as he tried to stand up in my pussy.

"Let me hear it, daddy. Tell me how this pussy feels," I said, humping into him.

"Go . . . good," was all he said as his dick seemed to grow inside of me.

"Fuck," Nico panted, picking up his pace. He wrapped my legs around his waist and picked me up like I weighed nothing. With my legs tightly wrapped around him, he gripped my cheeks and spread them. I wrapped my arms around his shoulders and stared into his eyes as he bounced me up and down on his dick.

I didn't want him to see the power of his dick, so I stuck my tongue in his mouth as I came. At the same time, I could feel Nico's dick explode inside of me. As we panted, Nico eased down to the carpet. He grabbed the comforter from the bed and tossed it over us. Nico wrapped his arms around me.

"Nico," I said, looking at the wall.

"Shh. Let's just enjoy the silence. And whatever you wanted to say, say it to me tomorrow."

I nodded, feeling like a woman instead of a gangsta bitch. In his arms, I felt appreciated. But my mind couldn't help but wonder why he was being so, so lovable. As my mind played tricks on me, Nico pulled me closer. I blushed, feeling his dick against my ass. If he was playing me for a fool, I wouldn't know. But what I did know was that I would give him the world—just as long as he kept putting out my fire.

Chapter 18

-Emmanuel-

"Thank you, Janice. I'm glad you came in when you did, or else I would've done something really terrible," I explained as I sat in the passenger seat of her car.

Janice exited the Dallas Police Department parking lot. I looked neither in the rearview nor the side mirrors as she did. That place was behind me, and I didn't plan on looking back.

"What were you about to do?" Janice asked.

"Honestly . . ." I said, then sighed. "I was about to tell them everything."

"Why?" Janice said, sounding upset. "So you could spend the rest of your life in a jail cell? Are you kidding me? What were you thinking?"

"I wasn't," I said, raising my voice. "I wasn't thinking at all. I had a plan when I went into that quiet, cold room. But then they showed me pictures of the crime scene."

"You should know how they play. They question you, they show you pictures—they want to make the suspect feel guilty," Janice explained.

"I know their schemes. I know. But this was different. This time, Janice, I wasn't the lawyer who could come in the room and save the day. Normally, the vics are people I've never met, so I have no emotional attachment to them. But Janice, you have to understand—when I saw those pictures, when I saw Hannah, it all came back to me. And I started to relive it all. The sound that came from Hannah as she took her last breath right in front of me . . . I just couldn't take it,

Janice. I just couldn't. I started feeling guilty, because I was."

Janice shook her head as she drove. "No, no," she said, pulling the car over to the side of the road. "Look at me, Manny," she demanded.

Tears began to well up, stinging my eyes like battery acid. I couldn't face her. The guilt was a physical weight, a lead vest pressing down on my chest until my lungs felt like they were collapsing. The shame wasn't just a feeling—it was a toll I was paying in real-time, stripping away every bit of the man I pretended to be

Janice reached out, her touch firm as she hooked her finger under my chin. "Emmanuel," she whispered, her voice a lifeline in the middle of my storm. "Look at me, please."

I faced her as tears began to fall down my face.

"Manny, don't you think for one second that you're guilty. Hannah's death is not on you. You weren't the one who murdered her. You didn't pull the trigger. We're going to get the ones responsible for her death. Even though the man who pulled the trigger is dead, there are still people involved walking around free. The woman who started this domino effect—she will pay. Angel will pay," Janice vowed.

"But how, Janice? How can we make her pay? We're not killers; we can't stoop down to her level to get even. I can't allow it. No, I won't allow it."

"You're right, we won't stoop down to her level. We're going to bring her to our level. A woman like Angel . . . she wants to be in control. She wants to be noticed, admired. She yearns to be on the throne. In order to be a woman on the throne, people have to respect and fear you."

"What are you getting at, Janice?" I asked.

"We have to make Angel expose her hand. It's probably eating her up on the inside, knowing she was the reason for Kendrick's downfall, but she can't tell anyone."

"So, what do you suggest we do? She won't talk to us. She tried to have us killed."

"You're right, she won't. But she's not looking to tell us—we already know, remember? We both know she set him up. We both know she killed his cousin. Kendrick, to her knowledge, has no clue. And she wants to be the one to tell him. She wants to sit in front of him while he's on the other side of the table, knowing she put him there. She wants to see the look on his face. His reaction would be her satisfaction."

I smiled. "You're right. Who better to tell him he was betrayed than the betrayer?"

"The only thing is, we will have to get Kendrick to help set her up. It'll be the only way to get it documented," she explained.

My smile faded. I knew without a doubt Kendrick would never see me or trust me, especially pertaining to Angel or his freedom.

"Janice, the last time I saw Kendrick, he walked out of the visiting room and didn't look back. I doubt he would agree to see me. And if he were to sit down long enough to listen to what I have to say, who says he would trust me? Hell, I wouldn't trust *me* if I was him, after all I did to him."

"Don't stress over it. I promise it'll all work out. First things first—we have to locate Angel, wherever she's at."

Chapter 19

-Angel-

After taking a deep breath, I opened my eyes to see Nico's arm draped over me. I smiled, knowing he couldn't see my excitement from where he was laying. Looking over my shoulder, I saw he was sound asleep. Slowly, I eased his arm off me. I stood to my feet, my legs feeling like putty from the extreme sex I'd just received.

I snatched the bedsheet up and wrapped it around my naked body. Quietly, I eased to the nightstand in search of Nico's phone. I couldn't remember seeing him with it last night. The stand was vacant except for his keys and his money clip with money folded inside.

I opened the nightstand drawer. There was a gun inside—a Glock 40. I picked it up and checked the magazine. It was full, minus the one in the chamber. Something else in the drawer caught my eye. It was a picture. I picked it up. I noticed Ken instantly. Nico was on the far left, and there was a Hispanic woman in the middle. I assumed it was Lluvia, or in Ken's case, Rain.

Flipping the picture, I read the written words on the back:

'*Never let anything come between us*' – Ken.

I laughed as I tossed the picture back in the drawer. The woman in the middle had been the thing to come between them. It was crazy how life had sent them a sign, but neither of them saw it coming.

"What's so funny?" Nico's voice startled me.

I closed my eyes tight, still holding the Glock in my hand. I had been caught slipping.

"Nothing, if you don't know," I said without facing him. There would be no way to read me if he wasn't able to see my face.

I heard his footsteps as he walked behind me. My body got chills as his hand rubbed up and down my shoulder. He reminded me of Ken with the way he touched me.

Nico nestled his chin on my shoulder as he wrapped his arms around me. "That's the only picture I have of us together. All of us. Before—" he said, then stopped.

"Before what?" I asked, the gun still in my hand.

"Before me and Lluvia started seeing each other behind Ken's back. In this picture, we were all just friends. Ken and her, too," he said, reaching for the photo.

"Can I ask you something?"

"Sure, anything," he responded.

"Out of all the women, why her? I'm sure women were probably throwing themselves at you. So, why Ken's woman? Out of all the women you could've had?"

"Because . . ." he said, letting out a sigh. He walked to the bed and sat down, staring at the picture of the three of them. Yet his eyes were only focused on one face. Lluvia's.

I placed the gun back in its place. Nico's sorrow assured me I didn't need it. "Tell me," I said as I sat beside him.

He sighed. His eyes were open, but I could tell his mind had traveled to place he wasn't used to visiting.

"When we were just starting out, me and Ken were learning the ins and outs of the game, so we were always around Turtle. He was our mentor. Because of that, we'd take business trips with Turtle to see Luis, the plug. This one time we go to see Luis, and his daughter is there. We always knew he had a daughter, but we'd never seen her. But this one day, she's just *there*. She comes into the room and steals the moment. Captivated everyone. At the time, I'm seventeen and they're both sixteen. But even at that age, she had the true power of beauty," he said.

I nodded, remembering the day Ken and I went to see Luis, and Lluvia stole the show just by walking to the table.

"Yeah, I know. She can be mesmerizing to the eye of the beholder," I assured him.

"For me, it was love at first sight. The way she controlled not just the room, but the beat of my heart. I knew she was the one. I just knew."

"But she liked Ken," I said.

"No, she didn't like either of us at first," he added.

"So, how did y'all become close then?"

"We were assigned to show her around. Lluvia wanted to go out—shopping, bowling, all that—but she didn't want her security with her. She wanted to feel like a regular teenager, not a kingpin's daughter."

"Oh, so the typical good-girl-gone-bad story," I pointed out.

Nico shook his head. "Nah. A *perfect* girl, gone bad," he said, standing up. "She had never ventured out of her father's protection, and we all knew that. What was supposed to be a day of fun turned into a full summer. Turtle used her vulnerability to get into Luis's good graces. He assured Luis he would protect her when she was with us, and for that, Luis gave Turtle the lowest prices anyone had ever seen. Turtle was already known in the streets, but with those prices, he became the Godfather of Dallas, then the King of Texas."

"So, when did she fall for Ken?" I asked.

"She didn't fall for him. She was tripped into his arms. Turtle and Luis put them together. Ken would be the next in line after Turtle, and Lluvia after her father. A marriage between them would solidify the legacies."

"So, where was your place in all this?"

"My place," he said with a heavy sigh. "For Ken, I was his right hand. But for Lluvia, my place was in her heart—hidden from the reality that we could never be together."

"Did Ken ever know how you felt?"

"He found out. And he took it to heart," he said.

"What did he do?" I asked.

Nico walked up to me and grabbed my hand. He guided it to his chest, right over his heart. Under his tattoos were the scars of his past—reminders of his mistakes. Two overlapping bullet wounds like an infinity sign. A mark that assured him it'd be with him through death.

I gasped as my fingers caressed the deep-tissue pain. "He shot you over her?" I asked in disbelief.

"No, he *killed* me over her," Nico said, sitting back down. "He flat-lined me. He took my life, and Turtle saved it. To this day, Ken doesn't know I'm still alive. Neither does Lluvia. Only me, you, Turtle, and Ron. To the world, I'm dead."

"Wow." It was all I could say.

"And that's why I owe Turtle my life—because he saved it. And no, I don't regret what I did. I just . . . I hate how they use women in their chess game. I know there are queens on every board, but if you pay attention, the queen is protected more than the king."

I stood up. "Get dressed."

Nico looked at me, confused. "Where we going?"

I wasn't sure I really wanted to do it, but he had already lost so much. He'd sacrificed even more. He was right about one thing: the queen got a lot of protection, but even a queen would sacrifice to keep her king alive.

"I'm going to resurrect you."

Chapter 20

-Kendrick-

Everything that I'd just heard on the news—everything I'd just seen—was all too much to put together. I watched the news segment and I understood what the newscaster had said, but my brain wasn't quite getting it. How did Bull end up with Emmanuel, my attorney? What was I really caught up in?

Then it came to me. Emmanuel's visit. He was really telling me the truth. Angel had indeed set me up. But that would only mean that Angel had gotten to Bull. She'd turned him against me. My young Bull . . . I'd raised him up in the streets myself. I gave him the name he had. The power and respect. The fear—he'd earned that on his own, but without my tactics, he wouldn't have been able to instill it properly.

"Kendrick Watson." The guard yelled my name, startling me from my daydream. Being a street nigga, it puts you on guard when people call your government name. It's like a danger from the past coming back to get its revenge.

I sat up in my bunk and looked around the cramped cell. Everyone was asleep. I looked toward the guard without saying a word.

"You have an attorney visit," the guard said. I looked at him, puzzled. I didn't have an attorney anymore.

"I don't have a lawyer anymore," I said.

The guard looked at the paper. "You're Kendrick Watson?"

I nodded.

“Then either you get ready to see the attorney that you don’t have, or I’ll let her know you’re declining the visit.”

Her? I wondered who was "her." “Okay, give me five minutes, and I’ll be ready.” The guard walked away without saying another word.

My mind was doing laps, running circles around who the woman could be. I broke my five-minute mark getting ready; I was in a rush to see who this woman was.

As the guard let me out, my mind went back to my old lawyer, Emmanuel, and everything he did to betray me. He was worse than an enemy. At least with my enemy, I can’t be mad at all the wrongs that come from them. But my attorney? Someone I trusted? Someone I placed my freedom on the line with? I know there’s a lawyer-client privilege, but there should be more. Lawyer-client trust. Fuck that—I would never trust another lawyer, male or female!

As I stood outside the visiting room, I looked through the small glass-framed window to see a woman standing with her back to the door. She rummaged through her briefcase as if she was looking for something important. She wore a gray skirt that was tight around her waist and ass. Her hair was long, flowing with dirty blonde streaks down her back.

I opened the door and walked inside. Hearing me enter, she continued to go through her briefcase as if she hadn’t heard me.

“I didn’t hire you myself, so if you weren’t hired by family of mine, then you can leave. I don’t want no pro-bono attorney that don’t give a damn about me. I’ve already been railroaded once, not again.”

The woman, upon hearing my voice, stopped moving. She turned to face me. As soon as I saw her face, I laughed. This had to be a dream or some cruel joke. First, I get a visit from Emmanuel, and now his secretary?

“What’s so funny?” she asked. Her facial expression was humorless.

Tears began to fall down my face as I continued to laugh. "Emmanuel knew I wouldn't see him, so he sent you—his secretary. Like it would make a big fuckin' difference."

The smile that was on my face disappeared. Anger had taken over, and my smile wouldn't be coming back. I balled my fists and slammed them on the table at the same time. My mood change caused the woman to jump.

I walked around the table and grabbed her by her white button-down shirt. Shoving her against the wall, I shouted, "Y'all think this is a game, huh? You and him, playing with my emotions after all you've taken from me. My life, my money, and my fucking freedom."

The woman continued to look past me toward the door, hoping or even praying that a guard would come in and save her. I could see the fear in her eyes; I could practically smell it, as if she had sprayed it on for perfume.

"What, you think I won't kill you in this bitch? Is that what he thought—if he sent you, that I wouldn't lay hands on you? Huh?" I had to catch myself from really laying hands on her.

I looked at her. She could've yelled and screamed as loud as she wanted, but she didn't. I couldn't figure out why. Her chest panted as she stared into my eyes.

"Is that what you do? You control women with fear? Yell and hit them when you want to get your point across?" she asked while I had her pinned against the wall.

"You don't know shit about me," I shot back, staring a hole into the woman who had grown a pair of balls in just a matter of seconds.

She snatched away from my grasp. "I know more than you think," she said as she fixed her shirt, doing her best to get the wrinkles out. "Why do you think your wife did what she did, huh?" she asked.

I froze. The question didn't just hang in the air; it wrapped around my throat. My eyes widened as a cold realization washed over me. The anger that had been fueling my muscles drained out, replaced by a sickening clarity. I looked at the secretary—really *looked* at her—and the dots started connecting in a way that made my stomach turn. It wasn't just about me being a bad husband. It was a play. A setup. My mind flashed to Angel, and for the first time, I saw the devil behind the smile.

"Exactly," Emmanuel's secretary said as I remained silent, the truth written all over my face.

"She explained how you would beat her and mistreat her. You drove her away. You made her miserable," she continued.

"Why are you here, huh? To tell me I was a bad, abusive husband? You think I don't know what I did every day? I do. But even after all that I did, I don't deserve what I got. I loved her, I took care of her, and this is my punishment." I found myself feeling tears fall down my cheeks.

My head fell forward as all the regret came pouring down on me at once. My shoulders felt heavy, like the burdens of being a man had finally shown their true weight. And then I felt more weight. But not just any weight—it was light. Like a hand. Her hand.

Chapter 21

-Janice-

I listened to Kendrick rant at me like I was the one who had placed him here. Yes, I was on the same defense team that had betrayed him, but I was only guilty by association. To me, I didn't deserve the same punishment.

The grip he had on my shirt made the fabric bunch up as he held it tightly. At first, I was scared for my life; I actually thought he would hit me. But as I looked deeper into his eyes, I noticed he was more afraid than I was. So, I used his fear as my escape.

I snatched away from his grasp. "I know more than you think," I said. I fixed my shirt, doing my best to smooth out the wrinkles he'd caused.

"Why do you think your wife did what she did, huh?" I asked him. He looked at me as if someone had cut his tongue out. *Exactly*, I thought. "Exactly," I shouted.

"She explained how you would beat her and mistreat her. You drove her away. You made her miserable."

"Why are you here, huh? To tell me I was a bad, abusive husband? You think I don't know that?" he shouted. "You don't think I regret what I did every day? I do. But even after all that I did, I don't deserve what I got. I loved her, I took care of her, and this is my punishment," he said. Then, out of the blue, tears began to fall down his cheeks.

I looked at him. I actually felt sorry for him. I could tell deep down he really loved her. It was the same look

Emmanuel had on his face when Hannah died in his arms—the look of true love. A look I've yet to receive.

His head fell forward. The floodgates opened as the tears fell harder. I hated seeing him like this—pain at my hands. Well, not mine, but Emmanuel's. Even though I was only guilty by association, I was still guilty. I played a part by not warning him destruction was coming. I had caused him pain by not screaming at him to watch out before he walked into the pit. I had seen it and didn't warn him. Therefore, I was guilty.

I found myself moving in his direction. As his head was hunched over, I reached out to him but pulled my hand back. I wanted to console him. To let him know that I was sorry for the role I played in his pain, even if it was a small one.

I reached my hand out again, but this time I laid it on his shoulder. His crying stopped as he felt my touch.

"It's going to be okay, Kendrick," I said, trying to make him feel better.

He looked up at me. His cheeks were wet; his eyes were red. The way he looked at me, it was as if I'd just reopened old wounds.

Kendrick jumped to his feet. He rushed me, pinning me against the wall again. "It's going to be okay? It's going to be okay *how*, huh?" he shouted, his face inches from mine.

He was right to be upset. His anger was staring right at me, but I didn't care. His anger was cute in a dangerous way. He had both arms over my head, keeping me in place. I could've moved, but I chose not to. I couldn't help but think about the night Emmanuel and I broke into Kendrick's home and he came back early. We had to hide under the bed while Kendrick and Angel had sex—well, from what it sounded like, they did more than that. The position he had her in that night made my pussy wet, and even thinking about it now, I felt hot.

I couldn't help myself. I snatched Kendrick by his prison shirt, pulling him into me. I caught him off guard as I kissed his lips, then stuck my tongue down his throat. I don't know what my mind was thinking, but my hands did whatever they wanted. I reached down to his dick. Whatever pain or hurt he was experiencing had vanished; his dick was hard.

Kendrick pulled back. He looked at me up and down as if he was examining if I met his standards or not. My back was against the wall. I didn't know what else to do; my emotions had gotten the best of me. I had already made the first move, and now I was worried it was the wrong one.

"You don't want to do this with me right now," Kendrick said, staring at me.

I didn't know what to say, so I just nodded.

"Okay," Kendrick said. He went to my briefcase, pulled out a manila envelope, and walked to the door. He tore a nice-sized piece from the envelope and covered the glass frame on the door. It was a risky move—a "blind spot" that would eventually trigger the guards' suspicion if they did a walk-by—but in this cage, privacy was a luxury worth catching a charge for.

As he faced me, I felt nervous all of a sudden. I was soaking wet and anxious—but super nervous. Kendrick walked up to me. He stared at me all over. He grabbed me by the neck and applied pressure. I felt a slight tinge of fear. He looked into my eyes and squeezed harder. My mouth opened, gasping for air. As it did, he spat into my mouth and released the pressure. I don't know why, but that set my pussy on fire. It was something I'd heard about but wasn't kinky enough to ask for. Yet, I liked it.

Kendrick forcibly turned me to the wall. He untucked my shirt and unzipped my skirt from the back. I could feel the cool air hit my lower back as my skin was exposed. Kendrick kissed my neck softly, then bit the same spot, making me wince. My skirt fell to the floor. My boy-short cut panties hugged my ass. I couldn't see what he was doing behind me, but if I had to guess, he was staring. I wasn't blessed like most African American women, but for a white woman, I had a bubble butt—one I flaunted proudly.

I heard Kendrick fumbling with something behind me. Then I felt his hands on my ass, then my panties. He snatched them to the side. Then he picked me up from the back and sandwiched me to the wall. He held me up like I was a feather, then slowly started to ease me down.

Then I felt it. His dick entering my pussy.

He moaned and grunted as he broke through my warmth. He filled me up and held his position. Once he got a good grip on me, he fucked me, hard. He pounded my pussy from a standing position, raising me, then dropping me back down on his dick. I never got a chance to see his size, but from the fullness I was feeling, I knew his dick was big.

"*Umph . . . ohh . . . shit.*" I did my best to hold my moans in. I didn't want to get caught having sex in a federal prison with an inmate—one who was supposed to be my client.

My body whipped around. My feet never touched the ground. Kendrick placed me over the table, my legs wrapped around him. I was sandwiched between the hard table and his hard dick. Both were causing me pain, but one was more pleasure than pain.

Kendrick grabbed my hair and wrapped it around his hand. He jerked my head back and slammed in and out of my pussy with long, deep thrusts. He was doing my pussy the same way he would do his wife's face; he was beating it. Abusing it. Making it feel pain.

The feeling was bittersweet. I was hurting, but at the same time wishing he could go deeper. I badly wanted him to spank my ass. I wanted to be punished. I was, in fact, guilty—even if it was only by association. Still, I was guilty. I wanted to be punished. I didn't want time served. I didn't want community service. And I damn sure didn't want probation. I wished the times were like they were in the early 1700s; I wanted my punishment to be lashes. But not by hand—I wanted to feel the lashes. To be left with marks. I wanted to remember my punishment. I wanted to learn my lesson, yet still do it again just to get more.

Kendrick forced my head forward, smushing it against the table. My cheek lay on the cold surface under his pressured hand. He rammed my pussy like he was trying to kill me. I didn't deserve the death penalty, but my pussy did.

"Punish me," I managed to say, my face smushed against the table. "Kill my pussy. Punish it, Kendrick. I deserve it. Take your anger out on my pussy. I've been bad. So bad." I shocked myself with my own words.

Kendrick took my words to heart. He pulled his dick out. He spat on my asshole and rubbed it into my crinkled hole. I thought he was only going to place his finger there, but then I felt the head of his dick poking at my back door. I had bitten off more than I could chew, but I had already signed the agreement.

Kendrick eased his dick in at first. I bit my bottom lip, trying my best not to scream. Once he was in, he forcibly started ramming his dick into my asshole. Tears fell down my cheeks as he pounded me. The pain was almost unbearable, but my pussy seemed to get wetter. I reached under me and massaged my clit as he rammed in and out of my back door.

"Ohh, punish me, Kendrick. I—I'm so sorry," I moaned as tears fell down my face.

Kendrick continued to pound my ass. I wasn't sure if he'd forgive me or not, but as he came inside me, he pulled out and slapped his dick against my ass. I came all down my leg as my body spasmed.

I lay over the table, unable to move. Kendrick slapped my ass, bringing a smile to my face.

"All is forgiven," he said.

Chapter 22

-Angel-

"Where to?" Nico asked as he sat behind the steering wheel of his car.

"Make a right at the next light," I said, pointing up the street. "He said he'll be parked by a black Lexus in an all-white van. Look for one with a ladder on top."

I peeped over at Nico. He followed my instructions, but I could sense he had doubts. Hell, I would too if the shoe was on the other foot.

"So," Nico said. "What do you think? Should I park next to his van, or what?" he asked as we pulled up to the pharmacy parking lot.

"Park next to the van," I said, a smile appearing on my face.

Nico nodded. He reached beside the seat and grabbed his Glock. On the inside, I smiled. I had to respect a real street nigga, and Nico was just that. He set his Glock on his lap as he pulled up to the van and parked beside it. Nico turned the lights off but kept the engine running.

The passenger door to the van opened, and out stepped my sister, Chelsea. I opened the door and jumped out. We embraced for what felt like minutes.

"Bitch, I was worried sick. People were running around saying you were dead. Girl, what happened?" Chels asked.

I waved my hand, trying not to think too hard about it. I wanted to forget that day and move forward with my life.

"Forget all that. I'm alive and I'm not going anywhere. Period," I said.

"Period, pooh," Chelsea added.

The driver's side door to the van opened. Trent, Chelsea's husband, stepped out. As soon as he did, Nico jumped out too, his gun in his hand but held at his side.

Chelsea looked at me with puzzled but approving eyes. She leaned to my ear and whispered, "Girl, who is *that*?"

I smiled. "Nico," I said.

"Why I never met him? Looking like he's Mr. Captain Save-a-Hoe!" Chelsea joked.

I laughed. "Trick, shut up."

Trent looked down at the gun in Nico's hand and chuckled. "Hey, sis," Trent said while hugging me.

"Hey, T. Thank you for everything, for real," I said.

"We family. We look out for each other," Trent said.

"And bitch, we better get some major, *major* paper, hoe. Got a bitch driving all over the city with Colombia in the back. Bitch, never again," Chelsea said, causing me to laugh.

"You know I got y'all," I said, then looked at Nico.

"Hey, stranger. You can't talk?" Chelsea said to Nico. Through all the tough act, Nico managed to bring a smile to his face.

"What's goody?" Nico said, all suave-like.

"So you my sis' new boo? You got big shoes to fill. Her last nigga was a piece of shit, but the man knew how to spoil a woman, huh, sis?" Chelsea said, then tried to high-five me.

The look on Nico's face confirmed my thoughts: he really hated Kendrick. I left Chelsea hanging. "Girl, fuck Ken. Next subject," I said.

"I'll do better than her last. I can assure you that. I can guarantee you, give me time and y'all won't even remember his name."

I smiled, hearing Nico claim me as his own. Chelsea couldn't help but smile, too.

"Okay, lover boy. We've been in this parking lot way too long. Give me your keys and we'll exchange cars. You can pick your whip up later. The van? Dispose of it once you're finished. The van is stolen, but the plates are clean," Trent explained.

"My car?" Nico said.

"Yeah, your car. I don't want it. And do us all a favor—tuck the strap. Ain't no need for it," Trent pointed out.

Nico felt so comfortable with his strap in his hand that he'd forgotten he had it out. He tucked the gun into his waist, looked at Trent, and said, "Don't scratch my shit."

Trent laughed. "Girl, let us go. You know how niggas are about their cars," Chelsea said as she hugged me.

"Later, sis. I'll call you once we make it," I assured her.

"Okay. And Jas said to tell you hey," Chelsea said as she opened the passenger side door.

"Why didn't she come with you?" I asked.

"Smurf. He keeps his claws in her. But when you get settled, we'll come by."

I nodded and blew her a kiss. Nico watched his car drive off like he was watching his only child head off to college.

"Chill, it's only a car. Plus, you'll get it back. Once we take care of this, we can get it," I assured him.

"It's not just a car. That was—" he said, then stopped. "The car holds a lot of memories, is all," he added.

Nico walked to the driver's side of the van. I laughed on the inside as I sat in the passenger seat. "How far are we going?" Nico asked.

"I don't know. This belongs to you, so take it where you feel safe," I said as I leaned back in my seat.

"It belongs to me?" he asked, confused.

"Yeah. All two hundred ki's," I said with a smile on my face. My eyes were closed, but without a doubt, I knew his eyes were on me.

Chapter 23

-Nico-

I did the dash as I drove to the nearest storage unit. As I parked, I walked up to the entrance of the facility. The lights looked as if they were off. I looked at my watch; it was a quarter til' six.

I pulled the door, but it was locked. I looked closer through the glass. The store seemed to be closed, even though the sign read that the main office didn't close til' six p.m. I didn't understand why the door was locked.

I turned around. I had to find a spot; I didn't want to be riding around with what Angel stated were two hundred kilos. I figured they were ki's, but I felt like she was exaggerating about the number.

As I opened the driver's door, I heard what sounded like a lock being turned. I looked over my shoulder to see the door being opened.

"Sorry, guy. I thought no one was going to come by this late, so I was already closing up for the night," a fat Caucasian male said as he held the door open.

"It's no biggie. I just need to rent out a unit," I said in a hurry.

"Okay. I'll need your identification card, and I'll need you to fill out these forms," he said, handing me a clipboard.

I patted my back pocket, then I looked back at the van. "Shit."

"Is there a problem?" he asked.

"I don't have my ID on me. I left it in my car. I won't have enough time to go home and get it before y'all close, and I really need a unit tonight. I can pay extra," I said, pulling out a wad of money.

The man's eyes got big as he saw all the dead presidents overlapping each other. "Uh-uh . . . I think I can help you. Just—just fill out the forms, and I'll handle the ID part."

I smiled. I pulled off a grand from my roll and slid it across the countertop. I grabbed the pen that was attached to the clipboard by some yarn. I filled out all the info, giving a false identity that I always used.

As I finished, I handed the guy the clipboard. "I really appreciate it. I'll come back tomorrow with my ID," I lied. I was only going to use the unit until tomorrow; I just had to find a more secluded place.

"No problem. Here's your copy of everything. I also threw in a free padlock. On me," he said, then smiled.

Yeah, right, I thought to myself. *On me, my ass. That grand paid for it.* But I played into his hands. "I appreciate it, my guy. Gotta have one of these. I'on know how I forgot it," I laughed.

"Do you need help?" he asked.

"Yeah," I responded fast, then checked myself. "No. I mean, nawl, I got it. Appreciate it though, really." I held my fist out. "You saved the day, Nick," I said, reading the name on his tag.

"Just doing my job. But thank you, Dontae," he said, calling me by the name I'd used on the application.

I hurriedly got to the van. I followed the signs that pointed me in the direction of my unit. I parked and jumped out. I threw the door up on my unit; it was empty as expected. I walked around to the front of the van and saw Angel. She sat in the passenger seat asleep. Looking at her, I could tell she was tired. From everything she'd been through, she deserved some good rest. That's why once we finished, I was going to put her up in a nice suite. Doll her up, show her my appreciation.

I looked at the pallet in the back. It was stacked high with something, but I couldn't see what was under it because it was covered with a black tarp. I looked over my shoulder to make sure no one was around. Once I saw the coast was clear, I raised the tarp.

I couldn't believe my eyes. Under the tarp laid stacks and stacks of cocaine wrapped in plastic.

My forehead instantly started sweating. I stepped into the back of the van and started tearing the plastic like I was a kid on Christmas Day opening up gifts. I grabbed the first kilo and tore a hole smack through the middle of it. I just had to be sure I had what I thought I had.

I used my pinky nail to scoop some of the powdery substance. I brought it to my nose, then decided against it. I placed the powder inside my bottom lip on my gums. Instantly, my gums went numb. My eyes shot open and became watery.

I looked at the stack of kilos. Angel had said there were two hundred total. I didn't have enough time to count them; I was in a hurry to get them out of the van. I started grabbing them two by two, piling them on top of each other as I carried them into the storage unit.

I don't know if it was all the trips back and forth or the effects of the powder, but I was sweating like I'd been shooting dice in hell. After about twenty or thirty trips—I couldn't really remember—I finally got it done and covered them with the tarp.

"Oh, you're still here?" Nick said, startling me. I yanked the door down.

"Yeah, I was just leaving," I said, trying to sound like I wasn't up to no good. I placed the lock on the door and snapped it shut. I yanked on it to make sure it was secure.

"What are you still doing here? I thought y'all closed at six. It's way past six," I said.

"Yeah, before I leave, I have to make sure no one is sleeping inside the units. People try to use them like homes," Nick laughed.

"Oh, okay," I said. "Well, I'm out." I grabbed the padlock plastic and got in the van.

As I closed the door, I looked over to Angel. She was still sound asleep. I leaned over and kissed her on the forehead. She was more than just an angel; she was my guardian Angel.

Chapter 24

-Janice-

I walked into my apartment. I had stayed at the office almost all day, doing my best to avoid Emmanuel after what I had done. Emmanuel had called me and asked if I needed any help; I told him no. I made him think that him being out would draw cameras his way and he didn't need any more attention on him. So, he stayed at my place all day.

"Hey, Janice, I'm in the kitchen," Emmanuel said upon hearing me come inside.

I set my keys on the stand by the door and kicked my heels off. I took a deep breath as I walked into the kitchen. "Hey, what are you cooking? It smells good."

Emmanuel had an apron on—one I had bought years ago for myself but never had time to use. Emmanuel kissed me on the lips.

"Lobster and garlic bread, with Caesar salads," he said. He looked me over. "You look beat. Long day?"

"You can say that," I said, *thinking about how Kendrick beat my insides up.*

"How did it go with Kendrick?" he asked, catching me off guard. I felt like he could read my mind.

My mind went to how strong his hands were. The grip he had on my neck. The way his thighs smacked against my ass. My ass . . . Oh God, the way he made me cum by massaging my asshole. I had never, ever felt my body do what it did. The sensational feeling of where we were fucking . . . just the thought of being caught had me wetter than I'd ever been.

"Janice," Emmanuel shouted my name, bringing me back to reality.

"Huh?" I said.

"Kendrick. How did it go when you went to see him?"

"Oh, yeah. I went," I said.

Emmanuel laughed. "I know you went. I said *how* did it go? Are you okay?" he asked, walking up to me.

I walked away just as he was getting close. "Yes, I'm fine. Like you said, I'm beat. The day was cramped."

Emmanuel grabbed a chair. "Take a seat. I know your feet must be hurting," he insisted.

I sat down. Not only were my feet hurting, but my mind was tired, too. It had been racing since the visit to the prison.

"So, tell me how it went," Emmanuel said.

"I went to talk to him, and in the beginning, he didn't want to see me. He remembered my face from the trial."

"And when he noticed it was you, what did he say?" Emmanuel asked.

"He actually threatened my life. He insisted that we were toying with him. He even laughed at us," I remembered.

Emmanuel laughed, finding it all funny. "Then what did he do?"

I sat quietly. *The feelings. The positions. They all came back.* I shook my head to get the images out. "He snatched me up," I told the truth.

"He did what?" Emmanuel shouted.

"He grabbed my shirt and shoved me to the wall." I relived the awkward moment.

"The nerve of him. Where was the guard?" he asked.

"I'm not sure. But you know they don't allow any guards in the room during attorney visits. So, it was just us."

"Why didn't you scream for help? Did he hurt you?" he asked.

I shook my head with my eyes closed. *He did hurt me, but in a good way. My asshole was sore, but a good sore.*

"No, he didn't hurt me. I talked him down, and he calmed down enough to hear me out."

"So, he went with the plan to set Angel up?" he asked, all excited.

"No, he didn't. Not exactly," I said.

"Then what?"

"He agreed to let me help get him out, but he said he didn't want to play any part in snitching. He had been set up before, so he said he could never do anyone like that—not even the woman that had crossed him out."

Emmanuel sighed. "So what? If he won't do it, then how will we get Angel to confess everything? If we don't get her to confess, then I'm as good as dead myself. I might as well be Kendrick's celly," he exaggerated.

"Calm down. Kendrick did say he had a way that you two can be clear."

"How?" he wanted to know.

"If Angel sees that you're alive, she'll do everything to kill you," I pointed out.

"What, so he planned to use me as bait?" Emmanuel scoffed. "That's insane."

"It can work. All you have to do is threaten her with telling the truth. Tell her you'll expose everything if she won't pay you more money. It could work," I said.

Emmanuel stood over the counter with his hands on it. "It could work, but she could also kill me. I've seen firsthand what she can do. She's the real deal, Janice."

I walked up behind him. I wrapped my arms around him from the back. "This is the only way. You have to. It's the only way."

He sighed. "Okay. I'll do it. I'll set Mrs. Angel up. But I just pray she doesn't kill me before we get the job done."

***

-Ken-

I laid in my bunk, thinking about the day I'd had. My life was insane—a movie, in a way. My lawyer . . . or should I call her "Lady Snow"? She said to call her Janice, but I preferred *Lady Snow*. I had heard a lot about being with a white woman. I hadn't slept with one before today, but from what I'd heard, everyone said that white women—"snow bunnies"—were real freaks. They'll let you do anything to them. And from what I'd experienced earlier, every bit of it was true.

Honestly, I wasn't an "asshole" kind of guy. But when she begged me to punish her, I felt like that was the only way. I can't lie; I thought she was going to shit all over my dick. She took it like a straight champ, though—I'll give her that. She had some good pussy, too. And a nice ass for a white woman. I couldn't help but smack her on the ass once I was done. Hell, the shit was so good, I even forgave the bitch, even though she only played a small part.

But once we sat and talked, she told me what she had come for. Emmanuel and her came up with a plan to get me to set Angel up on a wire, exposing everything she did—including killing my cousin, Dip. I wasn't no snitch, so I deaded that shit instantly. Plus, I wasn't no dumbass. There was no telling what Angel would say. She might expose me on more shit the Feds don't know, then I'll *never* get out.

So, I came up with my own plan. A plan to get me temporarily free. I knew I couldn't get out scot-free because they had me dead to rights on the dope case. I just wanted to get out long enough to take care of all the unfinished business I left behind.

So, I told Lady Snow what I needed from her, and she seemed to be on board with it all. When I was talking to her, she looked me in the eyes the entire time. *I think I turned her out.*

When Lady Snow left, I contacted Pistol and told him to get in touch with Angel. Tell her that I needed to see her—like yesterday. Pistol said no one had heard from her. Then, hours later, he hit me saying Smurf heard his girl, Jas, talking to Angel. I wasn't going to beg her to visit. I just asked Smurf to relay a message for me. He said he delivered it. Now, all I had to do was wait.

Chapter 25

-Angel-

I woke up in the parking lot of Renaissance Hotel. Nico parked the van. "You finally woke up, huh?" he smiled.

"What are we doing here?" I asked.

"I finished unloading everything. The entire time, you was sound asleep. I was going to go back to my place. But I figured you needed fresh sheets, room service, and some champagne."

I smiled and yawned. "Nigga, you going to need more than a hotel room to even out the score," I teased.

"That's why I got the penthouse suite," he smiled.

"I guess that's a start," I said as I opened the door. My phone chimed. No one had my number but my sisters, so I knew it had to be important.

I checked my phone to see I had a message from Jas'. She texted me that Kendrick wanted me to come and visit him. I looked at his name—the weight it carried, even from behind bars.

Nico opened the driver's side door. "Nico," I said.

"Yeah?" he said.

"I—I. Do you think I can be alone tonight? Please. I'm tired. like you said, I need to get some rest. I just want to go to the room and drink myself to sleep."

"You sure? I can come with you. That way you don't have to be alone. We don't have to do anything," he said, being a gentleman.

"It's not that. I just need myself right now. Peace and quiet, alone. I hope you can understand."

Nico walked up to me and wrapped his arms around me. "Of course, I understand," he said, then kissed me on the forehead.

"The room is already paid for. I called ahead while we was in the van. It's under the name Dontae Moore. Go get you some rest. I'll swing by tomorrow. Just hit me if you need me."

I looked up and kissed him on the lips. *I know for sure I won't be able to get any sleep tonight*. My mind was too occupied. I was going to be up all night trying to figure out what I would say to Ken at the visit.

***

I couldn't sleep at all, just like I knew I wouldn't. I stayed up drinking expensive liquor from the bar. I stayed in the mirror rehearsing everything I would say to Ken once I sat across from him.

I was like a rooster on top of the barn, waiting for the sun to come up so I could announce the new day. I called myself an Uber. I went to the mall and bought an expensive outfit. I got my hair and makeup done also.

I was the first one in line when visitation opened. I sat at the table awaiting Ken. Sad to say, I was nervous. No, I was nervous as hell. To say this man had an effect on me was an understatement. I looked around the room; there was only me and another woman who had come with two toddlers.

Seeing her with her kids made me think about us—Ken and me. There was so much to tell him. I just had to figure out how I would deliver everything. I wanted him to know that *I* was the one to fuck him over. I wanted him to know that *I* placed him behind bars. But I also had more news to share. I figured I'd say, *"Fuck you, nigga, I hope you never get out of prison, and when you do, your son or daughter will be old enough to hate you."* Yeah, I was pregnant. I knew it when my cycle didn't come. When Turtle kidnapped me, I thought I was just so scared that I missed it, but even after Nico helped me get away, it still didn't come. So, in the midst of me getting drunk last night, I got the courage to get a pregnancy test. I walked my goofy, drunk ass to the store. I bought two pregnancy tests, and lo and behold, they came back positive.

I looked up to see Kendrick. He walked into the room, escorted by a guard. He looked damn good in his prison get-up. Gucci, Tom Ford, or prison grey—he was still Big Ken. The man who stole my heart. Too bad I came to take it back.

"Damn, girl, you looking good," he said as he sat down in the seat opposite me.

"Uh-huh." That was all I gave him. He laughed as he scooted his chair closer to the table.

"I've been hearing a lot of hearsay in the streets. Looking at your demeanor, I guess I could say it's true."

"What do you want from me, huh, Ken?" I asked.

"I just want to hear it from you. The woman I placed a ring on," he said, looking toward my empty ring finger.

"As you can see, there is no ring anymore. And I don't know what you heard, so you tell me what's good." I played along.

Ken chuckled again. "I heard that you're the one who placed me here. That you off'd Dip and tried to plant the gun on my attorney. You blackmailed him into throwing the case so I could do the rest of my natural black life behind bars."

When he recited it all back to me, it sounded way worse coming from him. So I just sat there, not saying anything.

"Is it true?" he asked.

"Yes." There—I said it.

"Why, though, Angel?"

Why? Did he really just ask me, *why*? This nigga. After everything he put me through, he really asked me why.

"Nigga, you've got som' nerve. Why? Don't you remember all the ass-whoopings you handed out to me? All those mornings I spent in front of the mirror applying makeup to my black eyes and bruised cheeks? Applying red lipstick over my busted lips, hoping the colors would blend in together? Really, nigga."

Ken sat silently in his seat. Then he said, "You were better off killing me. I wouldn't wish this on my worst enemy, Angel. You placed me in a concrete coffin for laying hands on you? Really? I'd rather you stab me in my sleep or shoot me in the face. Prison . . . really? I thought you were better than that. We exchanged vows, Angel. For better or for worse."

The more he talked, the more I wanted to reach across the table and slap the shit out of him until my hand went numb. Maybe he was right. Maybe I *should've* twisted a blade into his ribs while he snored. Or tucked a .45 under his chin and painted the headboard with his brains. Then I wouldn't have to sit across from him here listening to him whine about a prison cell like it was worse than the cage he kept me in for years.

Prison, really? He was worried about those bars? I'd been doing a life sentence since the day I said "I do." He was worried about his freedom but what about mine? Just because the bruises had faded and the swelling went down didn't mean I wasn't still bleeding on the inside. My scars weren't etched in ink or jagged skin; they were branded onto my soul.

I jumped up from my seat; I was fed up with his shit. It was now or never. "I did everything you wanted. I put up with a lot of your shit. Yes, I got tired of being your punching bag. Do I regret it? Maybe. But what's done is done. I'm moving on with my life, Kendrick. And you need to find a way to do the same in this cage. I'm filing for divorce; it's already in motion. Whatever the Feds didn't strip from the house, I'm liquidating it. I'll put some paper on your books so you can eat, but don't expect a thank you note. I'm giving you this one last piece of me, and once it's out of my mouth, we're flatlined. Don't look for a heartbeat, Kendrick, because I already pulled the plug." I took a deep breath that felt like it was finally reaching my lungs for the first time in years." I sighed.

"I'm pregnant with your child. So, if you send anyone to me, know that you're killing your seed, too."

Ken sat there with a dumb expression on his face. I was just waiting on his ugly ass to say the baby wasn't his; I was going to lose it.

"Angel, sit down. Please," he begged. I was beyond pissed at him, but my ignorant ass still sat back down. "You're really carrying my seed?" he asked.

I nodded, doing my best to hold my composure. I could feel the tears building up.

"Damn, Angel. You supposedly got a bounty on your head, and you're carrying my seed."

"Bounty?" I asked. "By who?"

"No name, but word is that you still got those kilos that were supposed to go to Turtle's exchange."

"And what?" I spat.

Ken shook his head. "Angel, I'm not there to protect you anymore."

"I don't need your protection. I got a man who can protect me," I said, matter-of-factly.

"New man?" he wanted to know.

"Yeah." I smirked.

"Who? Bull's dead ass?" he said, catching me off guard. "You haven't seen the news? Kid is already six feet under. So I hope you're not relying on him."

I sat straight up. "Nope. His name is Nico." I waited for Ken to figure it out.

"Don't know any Nico," he said.

"Oh, yes you do. You know him real well." I toyed with him.

Ken thought hard, then said, "Nawl. Son is dead. I killed him myself."

"Oh, his big-dick ass is very much alive and well. You can thank your snake-ass Uncle Turtle for that."

Ken looked at me, worried. "Angel, you can't fuck with him. He ain't no good."

"Says the nigga that beat me for fun."

Ken sighed. "Angel, I know you're mad at me. But you have to believe me. He's not the one to rely on. You can't trust him. There's a reason why I shot him," he explained.

"Yeah, because he slept with Lluvia," I said.

Ken looked confused. "Is that what he told you? That I shot him over Rain?" He shook his head. "That's not why."

Now *I* was confused. "Then tell me why you shot him."

"I have to tell you from the very beginning. All the way back to the sandbox."

To Be Continued

Lock Down Publications and Ca$h Presents Assisted Publishing Packages

Due to an increase in the price of services we have increased our prices. The prices below reflect the price increase as of 11/1/24.

BASIC PACKAGE **$699** Editing Cover Design Formatting	**UPGRADED PACKAGE** **$1000** Typing Editing Cover Design Formatting Upload eBooks to Amazon Upload Paperback to Amazon
ADVANCE PACKAGE **$1,400** Typing Editing (line editing/content) Cover Design Formatting Copyright Registration Proofreading Upload eBooks to Amazon Upload Paperback to Amazon	**LDP SUPREME PACKAGE** **$1,700** Typing Editing (line editing/content) Cover Design Formatting Copyright Registration Proofreading Set up Amazon Account Upload eBooks to Amazon Upload Paperback to Amazon Advertise on LDP's Amazon and Facebook Page

***

Other services available upon request.
Additional charges may apply

Lock Down Publications
P.O. Box 944
Stockbridge, GA 30281-9998
Phone: 470 303-9761
Email: lockdownpublications@gmail.com

Submission Guideline

Submit the first three chapters of your completed manuscript to ldpsubmissions@gmail.com. In the subject line add **Your Book's Title**. The manuscript must be in a Word Doc file and sent as an attachment. Document should be in Times New Roman, double spaced, and in size 12 font. Also, provide your synopsis and full contact information. If sending multiple submissions, they must each be in a separate email.

Have a story but no way to send it electronically? You can still submit to LDP/Ca$h Presents. Send in the first three chapters, written or typed, of your completed manuscript to:

LDP: Submissions Dept
P.O. Box 944
Stockbridge, GA 30281-9998

DO NOT send original manuscript. Must be a duplicate. Provide your synopsis and a cover letter containing your full contact information.

Thanks for considering LDP and Ca$h Presents.

NEW RELEASES

BLOODLINE OF A SAVAGE 1-3
THESE VICIOUS STREETS 1-3
RELENTLESS GOON 1-3
SOULLESS GOON 1&2
BY PRINCE A. TAUHID

THE BUTTERFLY MAFIA 3
BY FUMIYA PAYNE

A THUG'S STREET PRINCESS 1&2
BY MEESHA

CITY OF SMOKE 1-3
BY MOLOTTI

GET IT IN SLUGS 1 &2
BY B. STALL

STANDING ON HER BUSINESS 1&2
BY DG SANTANA

STEPPERS 1,2&3
THE REAL BADDIES OF CHI-RAQ 1-3
BY KING RIO

THE LANE 1-3
BY KEN-KEN SPENCE

THUG OF SPADES 1&2
LOVE IN THE TRENCHES 1&2
CORNER BOYS 1&2
ONCE YOU GO GANGSTA
PROTÉGÉ OF A LEGEND 1- 3
BY COREY ROBINSON

TIL DEATH 3
BY ARYANNA

THE BIRTH OF A GANGSTER 4
BY DELMONT PLAYER

PRODUCT OF THE STREETS 1-3
BY DEMOND "MONEY" ANDERSON

MONEY HUNGRY DEMONS 1-2
BY TRANAY ADAMS

TRAP STARS
BY B. SHELLY

HUB CITY MENACE 1-4
BY J. WHITE

A THUGGISH PASSION 1&2
LAND OF DA HOOLIGANZ 1-4
KILLAZ ON STANDBY 1&2
FRESH OFF DA PORCH 1-3
SECURE DA BAG
AMBITIONS OF A SLIDER
FOR MY ENEMIES SAKE
SOULLESS GOON 1&2
FO'EVA ROLLIN 1-4
BY ASSA RAYMOND BAKER

THE LEVEL UP 1&2
BY LUXURY KING

HUNGRY FOR MONEY 1&2
SLIMBOS

QUEEN OF NAPTOWN 1&2
THA TAKEOVER 1-3
BY KEITH CHANDLER

DRILL CITY 1&2
BY ZAY'TOWVEN

LOVE ME OR LET ME GO
BY R. FACEY

SAVAGE DREAMZ
BY KING DAVID

MONEY AND DEAD HOMIES
BY DERRICK SUMMERS

WHITE BOYS
BY BANDEMIC

A THUGS STREET PRINCESS 3 Coming Soon
BY MEESHA

BETRAYAL OF A G 2
BY RAY VINCI

SAVAGE FAMILY EMPIRE 1&2
SOULLESS GOON 1&2
THE DIRTY SIDE OF MONEY 1,2&3
BY PRINCE

BY THE TRUCKLOAD 1-4 COMING SOON
T SOULLESS GOON 1&2
IPPIN' THE SCALES 1-4
BAD BITCHES WIT GUNZ 1-3
PROBLEM SOLVED 1-3
THE GIRLRILLA AND HER N*GGA
THE SINGLE LADIES
BY CHRISTOPHER "DIESEL" HORNEZES

AVAILABLE NOW

RESTRAINING ORDER 1 & 2
BY CA$H & COFFEE

LOVE KNOWS NO BOUNDARIES 1-3
BY COFFEE

RAISED AS A GOON I, II, III & IV
BRED BY THE SLUMS I, II, III
BLAST FOR ME I & II
ROTTEN TO THE CORE I II III
A BRONX TALE I, II, III
DUFFLE BAG CARTEL I II III IV V VI
HEARTLESS GOON I II III IV V
A SAVAGE DOPEBOY I II
DRUG LORDS I II III
CUTTHROAT MAFIA I II
KING OF THE TRENCHES
BY GHOST

LAY IT DOWN I & II
LAST OF A DYING BREED I II
BLOOD STAINS OF A SHOTTA I & II III
BY JAMAICA

LOYAL TO THE GAME I II III
LIFE OF SIN I, II III
BY TJ & JELISSA

IF LOVING HIM IS WRONG…I & II
LOVE ME EVEN WHEN IT HURTS I II III
BY JELISSA

PUSH IT TO THE LIMIT
BY BRE' HAYES

BLOODY COMMAS I & II
SKI MASK CARTEL I, II & III
KING OF NEW YORK I II, III IV V
RISE TO POWER I II III
COKE KINGS I II III IV V
BORN HEARTLESS I II III IV
KING OF THE TRAP I II
BY T.J. EDWARDS

WHEN THE STREETS CLAP BACK I & II III
THE HEART OF A SAVAGE I II III IV
MONEY MAFIA I II
LOYAL TO THE SOIL I II III
BY JIBRIL WILLIAMS

A DISTINGUISHED THUG STOLE MY HEART I II & III
LOVE SHOULDN'T HURT I II III IV
RENEGADE BOYS 1-4
PAID IN KARMA 1-3
SAVAGE STORMS 1-3
AN UNFORESEEN LOVE 1-3
BABY, I'M WINTERTIME COLD 1-3
A THUG'S STREET PRINCESS 1,2&3
EMBRACING THE LOVE OF A BOSS
BY MEESHA

A GANGSTER'S CODE 1-3
A GANGSTER'S SYN 1-3
THE SAVAGE LIFE 1-3
CHAINED TO THE STREETS 1-3
BLOOD ON THE MONEY 1-3
A GANGSTA'S PAIN 1-3
BEAUTIFUL LIES AND UGLY TRUTHS
CHURCH IN THESE STREETS
BY J-BLUNT

CUM FOR ME 1-8
AN LDP EROTICA COLLABORATION

BLOOD OF A BOSS 1-5
SHADOWS OF THE GAME
TRAP BASTARD
BY ASKARI

THE STREETS BLEED MURDER 1-3
THE HEART OF A GANGSTA 1-3
BY JERRY JACKSON

WHEN A GOOD GIRL GOES BAD
BY ADRIENNE

THE COST OF LOYALTY 1-3
BY KWELI

BRIDE OF A HUSTLA 1-3
THE FETTI GIRLS 1-3
CORRUPTED BY A GANGSTA 1-4
BLINDED BY HIS LOVE
THE PRICE YOU PAY FOR LOVE 1-3
DOPE GIRL MAGIC 1-3
BY DESTINY SKAI

A KINGPIN'S AMBITION
A KINGPIN'S AMBITION II
I MURDER FOR THE DOUGH
BY AMBITIOUS

TRUE SAVAGE 1-7
DOPE BOY MAGIC 1-3
MIDNIGHT CARTEL 1-3
CITY OF KINGZ 1&2
NIGHTMARE ON SILENT AVE
THE PLUG OF LIL MEXICO 1&2
CLASSIC CITY
BY CHRIS GREEN

GANGSTA CITY
BY TEDDY DUKE

BACK IN BLOOD
SEX, MURDER AND GOD 1&2
COUNTDOWN OF A KILLA 1&2
GUNS DOWN, BOTTOMS UP 1&2
BY LO-LIFE

A GANGSTER'S REVENGE 1-4
THE BOSS MAN'S DAUGHTERS 1-5
A SAVAGE LOVE 1&2
BAE BELONGS TO ME 1&2
A HUSTLER'S DECEIT 1-3
WHAT BAD BITCHES DO 1-3
SOUL OF A MONSTER 1-3
KILL ZONE
A DOPE BOY'S QUEEN 1-3
TIL DEATH 1-3
IMMA DIE BOUT MINE 1-6
DYING FOR LIKES 1&2
KILLA CREW 1&2
BY ARYANNA

A DOPEBOY'S PRAYER
BY EDDIE "WOLF" LEE

THE KING CARTEL 1-3
BY FRANK GRESHAM

THESE NIGGAS AIN'T LOYAL 1-3
BY NIKKI TEE

GANGSTA SHYT 1-3
BY CATO

THE ULTIMATE BETRAYAL
BY PHOENIX

BOSS'N UP 1-3
BY ROYAL NICOLE

I LOVE YOU TO DEATH
BY DESTINY J

I RIDE FOR MY HITTA
I STILL RIDE FOR MY HITTA
BY MISTY HOLT

LOVE & CHASIN' PAPER
BY QAY CROCKETT

TO DIE IN VAIN
SINS OF A HUSTLA
BY ASAD

BROOKLYN HUSTLAZ
BY BOOGSY MORINA

A DRUG KING AND HIS DIAMOND 1-3
A DOPEMAN'S RICHES
HER MAN, MINE'S TOO 1&2
CASH MONEY HO'S
THE WIFEY I USED TO BE 1&2
PRETTY GIRLS DO NASTY THINGS
BY NICOLE GOOSBY

LIPSTICK KILLAH 1-3
CRIME OF PASSION 1-3
FRIEND OR FOE 1-3
BY MIMI

TRAPHOUSE KING 1-3
KINGPIN KILLAZ 1-3
STREET KINGS 1&2
PAID IN BLOOD 1&2
CARTEL KILLAZ 1-3
DOPE GODS 1&2
BY HOOD RICH

BROOKLYN ON LOCK 1 & 2
BY SONOVIA

THE STREETS ARE CALLING
BY DUQUIE WILSON

STEADY MOBBN' 1-3
THE STREETS STAINED MY SOUL 1-3
BY MARCELLUS ALLEN

WHO SHOT YA 1-3
SON OF A DOPE FIEND 1-4
HEAVEN GOT A GHETTO 1&2
SKI MASK MONEY 1&2
BY RENTA

GORILLAZ IN THE BAY 1-4
TEARS OF A GANGSTA 1/&2
3X KRAZY 1&2
STRAIGHT BEAST MODE 1&2
BY DE'KARI

SLAUGHTER GANG 1-3
RUTHLESS HEART 1-3
BY WILLIE SLAUGHTER

GOD BLESS THE TRAPPERS 1-3
THESE SCANDALOUS STREETS 1-3
FEAR MY GANGSTA 1-5
THESE STREETS DON'T LOVE NOBODY 1-2
BURY ME A G 1-5
A GANGSTA'S EMPIRE 1-4
THE DOPEMAN'S BODYGAURD 1&2
THE REALEST KILLAZ 1-3
THE LAST OF THE OGS 1-3
BY TRANAY ADAMS

MARRIED TO A BOSS 1-3
BY DESTINY SKAI & CHRIS GREEN

TRIGGADALE 1-3
MURDA WAS THE CASE 1-3
BY ELIJAH R. FREEMAN

KINGZ OF THE GAME 1-7
CRIME BOSS 1-4
BY PLAYA RAY

FUK SHYT
BY BLAKK DIAMOND

DON'T F#CK WITH MY HEART 1&2
BY LINNEA

ADDICTED TO THE DRAMA 1-3
IN THE ARM OF HIS BOSS
BY JAMILA

YAYO 1-4
A SHOOTER'S AMBITION 1&2
BRED IN THE GAME
BY S. ALLEN

TRAP GOD 1-3
RICH $AVAGE 1-3
MONEY IN THE GRAVE 1-3
CARTEL MONEY 1&2
BY MARTELL TROUBLESOME BOLDEN

FOREVER GANGSTA 1&2
GLOCKS ON SATIN SHEETS 1&2
BY ADRIAN DULAN

TOE TAGZ 1-4
LEVELS TO THIS SHYT 1&2
IT'S JUST ME AND YOU
BY AH'MILLION

LOYALTY AIN'T PROMISED 1&2
BY KEITH WILLIAMS

KINGPIN DREAMS 1-3
RAN OFF ON DA PLUG
BY PAPER BOI RARI

THE STREETS MADE ME 1-3
BY LARRY D. WRIGHT

CONFESSIONS OF A GANGSTA 1-4
CONFESSIONS OF A JACKBOY 1-3
CONFESSIONS OF A HITMAN
CONFESSIONS OF A DOPE BOY
BY NICHOLAS LOCK

I'M NOTHING WITHOUT HIS LOVE
SINS OF A THUG
TO THE THUG I LOVED BEFORE
A GANGSTA SAVED XMAS
IN A HUSTLER I TRUST
BY MONET DRAGUN

QUIET MONEY 1-3
THUG LIFE 1-3
EXTENDED CLIP 1&2
A GANGSTA'S PARADISE
BY TRAI'QUAN

CAUGHT UP IN THE LIFE 1-3
THE STREETS NEVER LET GO 1-3
BY ROBERT BAPTISTE

NEW TO THE GAME 1-3
MONEY, MURDER & MEMORIES 1-3
BY MALIK D. RICE

CREAM 2-3
THE STREETS WILL TALK
BY YOLANDA MOORE

THE STREETS WILL NEVER CLOSE 1-3
BY K'AJJI

LIFE OF A SAVAGE 1-4
A GANGSTA'S QUR'AN 1-4
MURDA SEASON 1-3
GANGLAND CARTEL 1-3
CHI'RAQ GANGSTAS 1-4
KILLERS ON ELM STREET 1-3
JACK BOYZ N DA BRONX 1-3
A DOPEBOY'S DREAM 1-3
JACK BOYS VS DOPE BOYS 1-3
COKE GIRLZ
COKE BOYS
SOSA GANG 1&2
BRONX SAVAGES
BODYMORE KINGPINS
BLOOD OF A GOON
BY ROMELL TUKES

CONCRETE KILLA 1-3
VICIOUS LOYALTY 1-3
BLOODY MONEY BAGS
BY KINGPEN

THE ULTIMATE SACRIFICE 1-6
KHADIFI
IF YOU CROSS ME ONCE 1-3
ANGEL 1-4
IN THE BLINK OF AN EYE
BY ANTHONY FIELDS

THE LIFE OF A HOOD STAR
BY CA$H & RASHIA WILSON

NIGHTMARES OF A HUSTLA 1-3
BLOOD AND GAMES 1&2
BY KING DREAM

HARD AND RUTHLESS 1&2
MOB TOWN 251
THE BILLIONAIRE BENTLEYS 1-3
REAL G'S MOVE IN SILENCE
BY VON DIESEL

MOB TIES 1-7
SOUL OF A HUSTLER, HEART OF A KILLER 1-3
GORILLAZ IN THE TRENCHES
OOPS CRY TOO 1-3
THE DAUGHTER OF A CARTEL BOSS 1&2
BY SAYNOMORE

BODYMORE MURDERLAND 1-3
THE BIRTH OF A GANGSTER 1-4
BY DELMONT PLAYER

FOR THE LOVE OF A BOSS 1&2
BY C. D. BLUE

KILLA KOUNTY 1-5
TENDER 1&2
BY KHUFU

MOBBED UP 1-4
THE BRICK MAN 1-5
THE COCAINE PRINCESS 1-10
STEPPERS 1-3
SUPER GREMLIN 1-5
A GANGSTA'S SON
THE CONNECT'S SECRET
BY KING RIO

MONEY GAME 1&2
BY SMOOVE DOLLA

A GANGSTA'S KARMA 1-5
BY FLAME

KING OF THE TRENCHES 1-3
By GHOST & TRANAY ADAMS

QUEEN OF THE ZOO 1&2
BY BLACK MIGO

GRIMEY WAYS 1-3
BETRAYAL OF A G
BY RAY VINCI

XMAS WITH AN ATL SHOOTER
BY CA$H & DESTINY SKAI

KING KILLA 1&2
PAPER, ROCK, SNAKES
BY VINCENT "VITTO" HOLLOWAY

BETRAYAL OF A THUG 1&2
BY FRE$H

COUNTDOWN OF A KILLA 1&2
SEX, MURDER AND GOD 1&2
GUNS DOWN, BOTTOMS UP 1&2
BY LO-LIFE

FOR THE LOVE OF BLOOD 1-4
BY JAMEL MITCHELL

HOOD CONSIGLIERE 1-3
NO TIME FOR ERROR 1&2
REAL
BY KEESE

THE PLUG'S RUTHLESS DAUGHTER 1,2&3
REDEMPTION IN THE STREETS
BY TONY DANIELS

BORN IN THE GRAVE 1-3
CRIME PAYS 1-3
BY SELF MADE TAY

MOAN IN MY MOUTH
BY XTASY

TORN BETWEEN A GANGSTER AND A GENTLEMAN
BY J-BLUNT

LOYALTY IS EVERYTHING 1-3
CITY OF SMOKE 1-3
BY MOLOTTI

HERE TODAY GONE TOMORROW 1&2
BY FLY ROCK

WOMEN LIE MEN LIE 1-4
FIFTY SHADES OF SNOW 1-3
STACK BEFORE YOU SPLURGE
GIRLS FALL LIKE DOMINOES
NAÏVE TO THE STREETS
BY ROY MILLIGAN

PILLOW PRINCESS
BY S. HAWKINS

THE BUTTERFLY MAFIA 1-3
SALUTE MY SAVAGERY 1&2
BY FUMIYA PAYNE

THE LANE 1&2
BY KEN-KEN SPENCE

THE PUSSY TRAP 1-5
BY NENE CAPRI

DIRTY DNA
BY BLAQUE

SANCTIFIED AND HORNY
BY XTASY

BOOKS BY LDP'S CEO, CA$H

TRUST IN NO MAN
TRUST IN NO MAN 2
TRUST IN NO MAN 3
BONDED BY BLOOD
SHORTY GOT A THUG
THUGS CRY
THUGS CRY 2
THUGS CRY 3
TRUST NO BITCH
TRUST NO BITCH 2
TRUST NO BITCH 3
TIL MY CASKET DROPS
RESTRAINING ORDER
RESTRAINING ORDER 2
IN LOVE WITH A CONVICT
LIFE OF A HOOD STAR
XMAS WITH AN ATL SHOOTER

www.ingramcontent.com/pod-product-compliance
Lightning Source LLC
LaVergne TN
LVHW010935110826
845149LV00013B/2608